Lightning at 200 Durham Street

A Joel Franklin Mystery, Volume 1

Ron Finch

Published by Ron Finch, 2018.

This is a work of fiction. Similarities to real people, places, or events are entirely coincidental.

LIGHTNING AT 200 DURHAM STREET

First edition. May 23, 2018.

Written by Ron Finch.

Dedication

I enjoyed writing this book. Most the time it was fun. Occasionally, since I didn't understand the software, mysterious things would happen. I would say the wrong thing by accident and two hours of work would disappear. After a brief interlude of cathartic cursing, I would become rational again and attempt to find the problem.

One day, as I was talking to my computer in a dramatic fashion, I must have used the word 'but.' The idiot computer, of course, thought I'd said 'cut.' After half an hour spent searching for my missing text, I noticed the paste symbol had become prominent. Wow. One flick of my finger and I'd recovered two hours of work.

Fortunately, I do most of my writing on the third floor (the attic) and that prevents my verbal dramatics from irritating my wonderful wife. Which prevents me from being chastised on a regular basis.

I'm dedicating this book to my wife Gloria; for her patience, for her faithful reading of my rough copy, and for her occasional suggestion that something I mentioned wasn't possible in 1928. She's been a constant source of encouragement and on slow days I can still hear her say to me in a loving way: 'I've had no pages from you to read yet today.'

I'm also dedicating this book to my son David, who's taken my unvarnished prose and converted it into a presentable story. He's a truly great editor.

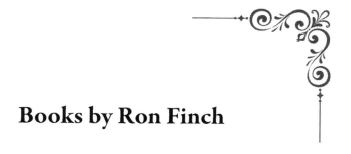

Books by Ron Finch

THE JOEL FRANKLIN MYSTERY Series:

Lightning at 200 Durham Street
Where's the Rest of the Body?

Important Quotes

"There are more things in heaven and earth, Horatio, than are dreamt of in your philosophy."

William Shakespeare

---~⌘~---

"Listen!"
Everyone's mother

---~⌘~---

"Believe nothing you hear, and only one half that you see."
Edgar Allen Poe

---~⌘~---

"Don't believe everything you think."
Allan Lokos

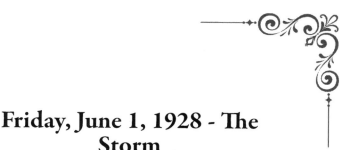

Friday, June 1, 1928 - The Storm

I COULD FEEL IT. JUST a sense. A whisper of dread in the sky.

Was it real?

There was definitely something. Very vague. Nothing specific. But I knew. I was uncomfortable.

Maybe the feeling would go away?

I hoped so.

I looked up from the book I was reading. From where I was sitting, I could see just above the railing of our front porch. Across the quiet street the large, three-story red brick Italianate house loomed. Evening was coming. To the east, the sky was darkening, but I saw no threatening clouds. But I could feel ... *something*.

Was it real? Why was I so uneasy?

I could just sense the edge of it.

Maybe it's just something in the air?

It was the time of year when things were stirring underground, occasionally peeking through to watch you with a wary eye.

I started to get up, but I didn't want to turn my back to the sky.

Why should I feel like this? Was I imagining it? It was just a sense.

It's getting cool.

That at least was real. That would be my excuse for going in.

Excuse to whom? To what? A sense? That makes no sense or nonsense.

But it didn't seem like nonsense.

3

I crossed the porch to the heavy front door. The latch stuck at first, but the door finally opened to an ever-darkening interior.

I'm in. I'm safe.

From what? Just a vague sense of uneasiness.

I looked up the curving staircase. Nothing. Just stairs.

I should put the light on.

I *needed* to put the light on. I needed to put *all* the lights on. Not to welcome anything, but to unwelcome things I didn't want to think about.

I slowly turned and looked to my left into the sitting room. I'd have to put the lights on in there as well. My good fortune: there was a lamp just inside the door.

I twisted it on. I could see the fireplace and my mother's dolls. They looked peaceful. But I could feel *something*. Just a sense. It had an unpleasant edge.

It was only 5 minutes to 8, but already it was very dark. The rest of the family would be home soon. They'd gone out to a family picnic at the church. I didn't go with them. I'm 17 and I had to mind the store. Right after school, I had to get down my parents' corner grocery store and look after business until 7:00 PM. The store is only open until 6:00 PM the rest of the week, unless there's an emergency, but it stays open an extra hour on Friday. If someone comes to the door of our home later on in the evening, then either mom or dad or I go to the store.

I didn't like being at home alone this particular night. I wasn't usually so nervous. There was something wrong. I could feel it. I had a foreboding sense of doom.

My room was in the attic. I liked it up there. Being the oldest, my mother said I deserved a space of my own. Mind you, there was a lot of stuff stored there, but there was room for my bed and the things that were important to me, and there was some light from a dormer window that faced almost southwest. At 5 foot 10, I could easily stand in the middle of the room, but if I grew to be as tall as some of my uncles it would be cramped quarters indeed.

I'll go up there. I'll feel safer in the attic.

I was a little worried about the second floor because it was very dark up there, but once I got the lights on I'd be okay.

The stairs talked to me all the way up. My dad had mentioned something about a mysterious two-way switch that involved some kind of ingenious wiring routine that allowed the hall lights to be turned off and on from downstairs or upstairs. I wished ours was like that. Fortunately, there was a light right at the top of the stairs. I turned it on.

It was still very dark in the house, but not as dark as the clouds I saw rolling toward me from the southwest through the window. I heard some rumbling and the roar of the wind. It was going to be a bad storm. I could feel it looming closer, feel the clouds humming with energy. Maybe that was just my imagination. I hoped so.

I made my way along the dimly-lit upper hall, past my sister's bedroom, then past my brother's bedroom, and through the second-floor sitting room to the attic staircase. It wasn't a very fancy staircase, but the 18 wooden steps took me up to my space in the attic. I was terrified. It was so dark, and I still had to get across the attic through the assorted piles of stored family stuff to the small light near my cot.

The storm was getting louder. Between the booms there was a crackling and an almost subliminal hiss. The lightning was closer, the wind higher, and those vague shapes in the attic more threatening than they had been on any other stormy night. I looked out the window, now very frightened. I was in the house by myself and in the path of what appeared to be a very wicked and peculiar storm.

It sounded like I was being cannonaded. The thunder was so loud and so continuous that I laid on the floor beside my cot and covered my ears with my hands. I didn't know what to do. I'd never heard a storm so loud. My ears were ringing. The only thing louder than the thunder was the raging beating of my heart. I was in animal mode, just wanting to hide and wait. The lightning was furious. The air itself seemed energized. And there was an odour. It occurred when the air was ionized. I'd read that in a book I'd borrowed from the library when I was doing an essay on electricity for my science class.

If the storm would have abated just a tiny bit, I could have gathered my courage, gotten to my feet, and gone down to the second floor, down to the first floor, and then down to our cellar. I might have been safer there. But there was no abatement. If anything, the storm had become more intense. It didn't seem possible. I was beginning to wonder whether the house would stand. I could see things blowing past the attic window. It wasn't a tornado, but it was an extremely strong wind. I just needed a tiny pause in the storm, a chance to escape from the attic, but at this moment all my energy was focused on staying rational.

Suddenly there was a brilliant light, leaving me momentarily blinded. The air seemed alive with electricity and strangeness. The roar was beyond deafening. There were other crashes, and in total darkness, just before I lost consciousness, I heard a strange man's voice shouting my name:

"Joel!"

Friday, May 11

"WHAT ANSWER DO YOU have for number six, Mr. Franklin?"

It seemed to me that Mr. Graf had spoken suddenly. I immediately stood up.

"Sir," I said, proud of myself for paying attention, "the answer is 17.2."

In reward, Mr. Graf said: "Mr. Franklin, this is not a game of horseshoes. 17.2 is not good enough. 17.2 is just a leaner. Mr. Franklin, please sit down. Let me see. Who thinks they have the correct answer? Mr. Jay Jarvis, what answer do you have?"

Jay, trying his best not to look smug, said: "Sir, I believe the correct answer is 17.2 *square centimetres.*"

"Mr. Jay Jarvis, you are correct." Mr. Graf turned to me. "Mr. Franklin, do you see the error of your ways?"

"Yes, sir," I said. "My answer wasn't accurate enough. I omitted the units."

"In mathematics, Mr. Franklin, you must be accurate. In this discipline you have a choice: you can be right, or you can be wrong. Things are not grey or off-white; they are correct or incorrect. Best you remember that, Mr. Franklin."

It was a hard thing to forget in Mr. Graf's class. Everyone had heard this theme – and slight variations on it – on a regular basis.

I sat down sweating. It wasn't hot, I just wasn't very good at handling public embarrassment. It was something I would have to work on. Especially if I planned on going into politics. I was certain Mr. Graf didn't think of it as an embarrassment; he was merely trying to educate me. I like mathematics, but sometimes I'm not the best at remembering details. Sometimes my mind wanders. And sometimes what I'm thinking about is much more interesting than what's going on in class. I think Mr. Graf believes that there's no room in the black-and-white world of mathematics for humour. I enjoy humour, which means I don't always enjoy his class. On the other hand, my friend Jay Jarvis seems to enjoy it. At least, he seems to enjoy following my incomplete answers with his own correct ones. Jay's a clever fellow, and he's my friend, but sometimes he's an ass.

I should probably tell you now what makes Jay special; that is, why Mr. Graf uses his first name in class. Jay's first name is not Jay. It's Joseph. Up until this year everyone called him Joe. But this year, on the first day of trigonometry class, Mr. Graf asked Jay Jarvis to answer a question. The class at first had not been certain what had happened. Was there a Jay Jarvis in the class? It had soon become apparent, however, that it was Joe who was being asked the question. When Joe had attempted to correct Mr. Graf – a brave but foolish act – he'd been informed that there were two boys with the same last name in the class, and since his first initial was J, he would be referred to from hereon as Jay Smith. That had ended the discussion. Since that time, everyone calls Joe Jay. Mr. Graf likes having an organized universe. Many in the class have pondered what naming system Mr. Graf would use if he had three or four young gentlemen or ladies with the same surname. It was a challenge we were certain Mr. Graf would rise to.

Actually, the latest part of the curriculum on trigonometry was interesting. It was easy to see the practical applications. One day earlier that week, the class had gone out to the football field with stakes, twine, marker cones, and a big blackboard protractor. (A surveyor would have laughed.) Our assignment for Mr. Graf had been to determine, using a baseline and a couple of angles, just how far away a cone at the end of the field had been placed. The class had been split into teams of two, and Jay and I had gotten to work together. It had been a nice afternoon, we'd been outdoors, and it had been fun as long as we weren't clowning around too much and drawing the ire and caustic remarks of Mr. Graf. The class had been far enough along in the trig application part of the course at the time that we'd had some formulas to work with, so Jay and I had set up a baseline. We'd used the entire width of the 10-yard line. That had given us a baseline 65 yards, or 195 feet, long. Then we'd sighted on a cone that we'd placed down the field about 2 yards wide of the rightmost goalpost. We'd known the answer had to be about 100 yards since the playing field is 110 yards in length. It had been a good exercise and a math class we'd both enjoyed.

But enough digression. The class was in progress, and Mr. Graf likes everyone to pay attention. I didn't get all my homework done and I preferred to leave at the regular time. I was expected home promptly after school to help in the store and I didn't want to have to dream up an alibi for my parents.

"Mr. Franklin, are you with us here in this classroom, in this school, on this planet? You seem to have drifted away," said Mr. Graf. "Focus yourself. One more lapse and you will have to stay after school. I have many interesting mathematics questions that you can work on that will help you focus."

"Sorry sir," I said hastily. And I meant it. I wasn't in favour of enjoying the privilege of Mr. Graf's company after school.

The class continued in a relatively uneventful way. At least uneventful for me. I had one more opportunity to answer and I did so correctly this time, remembering to include the units in my answer. Mr. Graf was pleased to see his educational efforts rewarded. Though Mr. Graf had caught a few people that day who did not have exact, all-inclusive answers, he was making progress; according to the tick marks he was making beside student names, the number of acceptable answers was increasing. In its own way, Mr. Graf's method was clever: he didn't get volunteers very often, but he did have a quiet classroom. No one wanted to be the focus of attention. All in all, in a begrudging way, we did learn our mathematics and our listening skills improved. Also, *most* of us did our homework.

WITH ABOUT FIVE MINUTES to go, Mr. Graf announced: "Please pay careful attention. I have an important assignment for you. It will be worth 25% of your term mark. Please take your pen and on a piece of paper jot down what is required. If you have questions, please stay at the end of the day and I will answer them.

"Your assignment is as follows: you are to produce a field report based on the outdoor trigonometry exercise we did on Tuesday. Recall that it involved using a baseline and angles to determine the distance to an object. You are to select a local landmark. The choice is up to you; establish your baseline, measure the angles, and determine the distances from both ends of the baseline to the landmark. This is a practical opportunity to use some of the trigonometry you have been taught. Your written report will be in the form of a scientific report and will include purpose, method, observations, diagrams, and conclusion. You may work on your own, or you may collaborate with a partner.

"I hope you have jotted all this down as it is extremely important to concisely state the purpose of this assignment, or, for that matter, any other venture you may take on later in life. This report is due on or before Tuesday, May 21st. Class dismissed."

It was the final class of the day so there was time for a bit of a hubbub. It was the first time anyone could remember anyone staying voluntarily past the bell. The big question was: what landmarks were we supposed to use? We wanted a list of specific sites, but Mr. Graf said:

"You will determine the landmark yourselves. It could be a bridge, a tall building, a large tree, or any other suitable object. It could be any number of things. I will determine whether you have made an appropriate choice when you hand in your assignment."

With that, everyone was out the door. The weekend beckoned.

The assignment was a surprise. It was the first out-of-class field assignment that Mr. Graf had given us. As a matter fact, no other teacher had ever given us this type of assignment before. We were used to homework assignments based on textbook questions or readings, but this was new to us.

"This almost makes me feel kind of grown up," said Jay, excited. "It's almost like an adventure."

"Don't get carried away," I said. "We're not the Hardy boys. This is just another kind of homework."

"Hey Joel, you'll enjoy this despite yourself," said Jay.

Most students have obligations after school. Chaseford is not that big a town – the population is still under 10,000 – so everybody either walks or bikes to school. Some kids from the country board in town during the week. Jay and I and our friends Georgie and Sylvia live in the same part of town, so we usually walk home together. It gives us time for chitchat.

Jay and I are both 17. We both do well in school. The similarity ends there. Jay is a more outgoing person than I am. I have a medium build, with blond hair and blue eyes, and trying my best to be 6 feet tall. Jay is about 3 inches shorter than me. He's also broader, stockier, and stronger. His black hair and brown eyes go well with his darker complexion. We've been best friends since I moved into the neighbourhood several years ago. We're always joined on our walk home by our good friends Georgie Harkness and Sylvia Grayson. Georgie's a tall girl with auburn hair. Sylvia is much shorter, maybe 5 foot 2, with blonde hair and brown eyes. The girls are both 16 years old. The four of us have been friends all through high school.

I started today's conversation by saying: "So, Jay, do you want to team up with me on this trig assignment?"

"Sure," said Jay. "Sometimes two heads are almost as good as one. Depending on who the heads belong to."

"That's a pretty weak attempt at a joke," said Georgie. "What assignment are you talking about?"

Georgie lives just two doors down from me. Both of our families have lived on Durham Street for more than 10 years. Georgie isn't always on the best of terms with Jay. She's told me a couple of times in the past that Jay thinks he's smarter than the rest of us. But the real difference is that Jay is very confident and not very polite.

"Mr. Graf gave us an assignment in class today," I explained. "To use what we learned in trigonometry in a practical way. We have to determine the distance to a landmark without measuring it directly. Our first big problem is to decide what landmark to focus on. Once we decide that, we can do the measurements and complete the assignment."

"What do you mean by a landmark?" said Sylvia.

"Just something that stands out on the horizon," said Jay. "Something that people would notice as they walk or drive through town, or drive through the countryside. It could be the town hall, for example, which is the tallest building in town."

"Let's not go with that," I said. "Let's try to find something a little more original. Any suggestions?"

"Maybe the flagpole in front of the library?" said Georgie.

"What about that real tall monument in the cemetery?" said Sylvia.

We kicked the idea around some more as we covered the next three blocks, but nothing really seemed to stand out so we switched topics.

"I'm probably going out to visit my cousins on Sunday afternoon," said Georgie. "It's not that far. They only live about 12 miles away, near Goshawk. Just on the south edge."

"You know, there's a very large bush near there," said Jay. "I have relatives out that way, too. They own some of that bush land."

"That's kind of a scary bush," said Georgie. "It's very dense. There seems to be a hill in the middle of it with a big tree on it. The top of the tree stands above everything else."

"You know what?" Sylvia interrupted excitedly. "Maybe that big tree is a good thing to use in your assignment? I don't imagine anybody else will think of it. Maybe you guys will get a bonus mark!"

"Great idea! Let's do it!" Jay and I said at the same time.

Saturday, May 12

EVERY SATURDAY, I WORKED in my parents' grocery store. **Franklin's Groceries** opened at seven in the morning and closed at six. I usually worked with my dad in the morning. That was our busiest time of the week. I got a lunch break from about noon until 12:30 while my dad served the customers. Then dad headed home for his lunch. My mom came in usually from 1:00 PM to 3:00 PM to help, then I was on my own until 6:00 PM, when I locked up.

It wasn't too bad. The mornings were usually very busy, with people getting ready for Sunday dinner and maybe company on Saturday night, as well as groceries for the week. Business usually died off about an hour after lunch time and by two in the afternoon things slowed down a lot. My mom mainly came in to check on me and see if there were any problems. My brother Ralph came in occasionally on Saturdays if we were really busy. Ralph was 12 years old and a very good athlete. Baseball took up most of his Saturdays during the summer, but he was gradually being introduced to the business.

Our parents were really good to me, my younger brother Ralph, and my baby sister Emmylou, who was 8. They tried to think of everything. They'd set up a little cubicle in the store, at the end of the row of canned goods, where I could sit down and work on my homework on Saturday afternoons when business was slow. It was a great location because, if someone came in, I was facing the door. Of course, the rule was that I had to be on my feet as soon as I heard the bell ring that let us know the door had been opened. Then I was up and greeting customers with a smile. The smile was also a rule.

That Saturday afternoon, just after my mom left, at about ten minutes after three, Jay came in for a visit. I wondered if he'd been watching the door, waiting for my mom to leave. I was happy to see him. Conversation with Jay beat working on my English essay.

"Are you ready for a Hardy boy's mystery?" he said.

"What are you talking about, Jay?"

"You know, the Trigonometry Bush Mystery."

I smiled. "You mean the Trigonometry Bush Misery?"

Jay smiled at that. "We need to make plans for tomorrow afternoon if the four of us are going to go," he said. "It's a Sunday, so we're going to have to be very persuasive. I told my parents how important the assignment is. I said your parents will probably okay our expedition, since it's school related. My mom knows how important education is to your mom, Joel. And it's supposed to be a beautiful afternoon. Maybe we can make a picnic out of it? I hope Georgie and Sylvia can come."

"That idea has good possibilities. There's just one problem," I said. "The location isn't very handy."

"That's not a problem," said Jay. "If you get permission from your parents, my dad says he's willing to take us out in the used car he bought last week. He's pretty excited about it. It's a 1925 Flint E 55. It was built in Flint, Michigan. Nice car with lots of room. It has a six cylinder Continental engine. New, they go for about 1200 bucks. I know that's kind of expensive, but my dad got his for just a little under $600. I'm really hoping to drive it soon. Remember, I have relatives out there. I think my dad wants to show the car off to my uncle Herbert. My uncle owns part of that Bush the big tree is in."

"Okay," I said. "Now it's up to you to find out if Sylvia can go. Remember, Georgie's supposed to be visiting her relatives out that way anyway, so maybe our plans will work out."

"Sounds like a plan," said Jay.

"I'll get in touch with Georgie and you get in touch with Sylvia," I said.

We agreed to meet again that night at about 8 o'clock, after supper, to make sure we had everything we needed for the assignment, and to see if our plans had fit together. With that, Jay was out the door and on his way.

That night, after supper, at about 7 o'clock, I went down the street and knocked on Georgie's door. I had a nice chat with her parents and then Georgie appeared. Georgie and I had been friends for a long time and her parents think I'm an okay kid. Actually, a 'fine young man', in their words. So they trust me.

They talked a bit about the trip to their relatives out near Goshawk the next day and about the possibility of Georgie meeting us at Jay's uncle's farm. I told them a bit about the assignment and that we were hoping that we could make a picnic out of it, too. Georgie was excited. Her parents agreed that Georgie could go on the picnic with us. They said they thought our plan would work. Jay's uncle Herbert's farm was one concession from the road where Georgie would be visiting her relatives and was only about a mile away. The plan was for Georgie to use one of her cousins' bikes and bike over to Herbert's farm. She would meet us there at about 2:00 PM. So far so good.

I went home.

When Jay appeared at my front door, he was carrying some kind of angle measuring device. It was easy to tell that this was something that Jay had concocted, or, as he would say, 'invented'. It was composed of a small protractor attached to a couple pieces of 1x2 about 2 feet long. He deserved credit for ingenuity, but the workmanship could be improved. In any case, it looked like it might work. Jay told me he had a big roll of rope at home. It was 300 feet long. He also had a couple of sturdy wooden stakes. Jay's dad ran a small construction company and he'd agreed to supply the rope, the wooden stakes, and a small sledgehammer.

"Did you find out if Sylvia could go?" I said.

"Yeah. Her mom and my mom have been very good friends since high school, so she can go. As a matter of fact, she's going to go in the car with us. Dad will pick her up."

I told Jay about Georgie and how she was getting there.

Now our plan was in place. We would all meet at Herbert's farm at 2 o'clock. We would head off from there to do the measurements and have a little bit of a picnic. It seemed like we were going to have a great Sunday afternoon.

Sunday, May 13

CHURCH AND SUNDAY SCHOOL were over. We made it home by 12:45, then we had a light lunch made from yesterday's leftovers. Reheated meat pie and potatoes, followed by some early fresh strawberries from the back garden. It made for a delicious meal.

Our garden was doing well. My brother Ralph and my sister Emmylou helped quite a bit. It was part of their after-school chores. It was a large garden for a town. We had a double lot, 132 feet wide by 166 feet deep. Our house, which was two stories plus, sat on one lot. The other lot was dedicated to the garden. This garden provided hours of entertainment for my younger brother and sister. The reward was lots of fresh vegetables and berries. We planted a little bit of everything in that garden, including a scarecrow.

"What time are you going out this afternoon?" asked my dad.

"I'm pretty sure Jay and his dad, and maybe Sylvia, will be here a little after 1:30," I said.

It was already 1:15 and I was ready to go. I usually had Kitchen Patrol – or KP – duty Sunday at lunchtime, but I had talked my younger brother Ralph into switching with me. He's quite an astute bargainer. It cost me two KP duties next week.

Just then, I heard a knock on the door and heard my dad say: "Hi Jay. How are you this afternoon? Is that your dad out there with his new vehicle?"

With that, my dad was out the door and in a conversation with Jay's dad about the car.

"That's a pretty nice looking car you have there, Brad. It's a Flint's isn't it? There aren't too many of those around. They built a really good product at a reasonable price. But if memory serves me right, the company went out of business last year."

"You're right," said Jay's dad. "The price was too enticing for me to refuse. And I happen to know that the Flint Company was taken over by Durant Motors, and they say they have lots of replacement parts stockpiled for repairs if local garages run out of them."

"Well, it's a great looking car," said my dad. "And it looks like you've got everything ready to go this afternoon. Except for Joel."

With that, I was out the front door, over to the car, and into the back seat with Sylvia and our supplies. Jay sat in the front with his dad. I think he was hoping to drive today. He's had his beginner's license for a few weeks now and has been driving regularly with his dad beside him in the front seat. I hope his dad's blood pressure medication does its job. Jay's positive comments about the car and his good behaviour over time will give him an opportunity at driving the Flint.

We took the main street out of Chaseford, which became Highway 8 past the edge of town. We drove out about 3 miles, turned right down a major concession road, and headed for Goshawk. Goshawk's just a village but there's lots of good farmland around it. We went through Goshawk to the first corner outside of town and turned left, then proceeded about two concessions. At the beginning of the next concession we were at Jay's uncle Herbert's farm. There, just beyond the farm, was the bush looming up above everything and stretching out along the road for some distance.

We pulled into the barnyard and circled around to the large porch that ran along the side of the big two-story farmhouse. Then we all climbed out of the car.

Jay's uncle Herbert came out to greet us. He told us aunt Emeline was busy in the house baking pies. Jay's aunt was renowned locally for her baked goods and thoughts of warm pie momentarily distracted me from the task at hand. Even before introductions Sylvia blurted out:

"Where is that big tree? All I see is a very large woods."

Uncle Herbert looked at us. "You must've just escaped from town. I guess you don't know too much about the countryside. From this farmyard, you are far too close to the woods to be able to see anything but the tops of the nearest trees."

"I'm sure I saw that tree when I drove by with my parents a week or two ago," said Sylvia.

"I'm sure you did, too," said Uncle Herbert. "From one concession over. There's a bit of a rise along that road. It's highly visible from there. So don't take your project supplies out of the car yet. I think you're going to need to set your stakes up one concession over if you want to be able to focus on that large tree."

Our plan had been perfect up until now. Now we'd encountered a minor flaw. A problem that we were able to solve with practical advice from Jay's uncle.

Jay's dad smiled and said: "I think that rise that Herbert was talking about starts just about one farm past where Georgie's relatives live. When you do your project, you're going to be a lot closer to Georgie's relatives farm than you are to this one. Get back in the car. I'll drive you over to Georgie's relatives and then to the rise in the road."

Jay's dad turned to Herbert. "I'll need a little time to drop these guys off and then I'll come back and visit with you. I'll let you tell me what a terrible year you're having on the land, despite what appears to be lush growth of all your crops. Then you can admire my car while I tell you what a great vehicle it is and what a good deal I made."

They both laughed. They knew there was just a touch of truth in what he'd said.

Georgie appeared on the bike that she'd borrowed from her cousin just as we'd gotten back in the car. She stopped at the entrance to the lane, smiled, and waved hello. This sent a chill through me. I knew that sunny smile was about to change into a storm cloud.

Georgie biked up to the car. I readied some words I felt I might have to use again from time to time, and, before anybody could say anything, I said: "Please let me explain."

"Explain what?" said Georgie, the first hint of a frown crossing her smile.

Sylvia stepped in to rescue me. She explained that the tree wasn't visible here because we were too close to the woods and that we would have to go back to the rise in the next road. The road that ran right past her cousin's place.

Georgie continued to look at me. Her smile was gone, her eyes had hardened, the storm was approaching, and I was very uncomfortable.

"Your plan seems to have a flaw in it," she said. "I biked all the way here and now we're going back to where I started?"

Rather than risk more hot tongue and cold shoulder, I said: "Guilty as charged. Please let me explain."

"I didn't like your first explanation," she snapped.

"Okay," I said. "How be you ride back in the car and I'll bring the bike?"

"That's an improvement," she said, somewhat mollified.

Everyone else chuckled. I was the centre of attention but I wasn't enjoying it. Georgie got in the car and I got on the bike. I knew that, secretly, she really wanted a ride in the Flint.

Off we went. I began to trail further and further behind as the Flint picked up speed. We stopped briefly at Georgie's relatives to explain what was going on and there I enjoyed another dose of embarrassment. I guess it was good for me: what doesn't kill you makes you stronger. Anyway, it was great to hear the laughter of lots of people. I just wished it hadn't been at my expense.

We bid Georgie's relatives goodbye and Jay's dad delivered us and our equipment about another mile up the road, just over the rise. From there, you could really see that large tree in the middle of the bush. We decided to call it Trigonometry Bush, or TB, for short. It's our inside joke.

Jay's dad dropped us off. It was now about 2:45 in the afternoon. He said he'd come back and pick us up at about 4:30 at Georgie's relatives, then away he went, back to visit with his brother-in-law in his Flint.

NOW WE COULD GET TO work.

"Remember," said Jay, "Mr. Graf told us to make a rough sketch before making any measurements. He said it was important, whenever possible, to make sure that your baseline was hopefully at least as long as the distance the landmark appeared to be away from you. So let's think about this for a couple of minutes. How far away would you think the big tree is?" Before we could answer, he continued by reminding us: "We're now about one concession from the edge of the bush. So that's a mile and a quarter at least, and that big tree appears to be back in the bush quite a ways. Seems to me my uncle told me that that concession behind his farm doesn't go all the way through the bush. The road ends in a T-intersection just before the bush. So, from here, it looks like the bush extends probably at least to the concession after that. So that tree is quite some distance from here. If that tree is in the middle of the bush, that would be about two concessions from here, or about two and a half miles."

Georgie looked at us and said: "That's not good news."

It suddenly dawned on me what was going on and why Georgie was concerned. If that tree was two and a half miles away, then our baseline should be at least a couple miles long. This was just another small hitch in our plan.

"Maybe we should have added bicycles to our equipment list," Jay chimed in, helpful as always.

"Great day for exercise," I said to my frowning friends. "Let's get at it. We're going to be doing some walking, and we won't have a lot of time to spare before Jay's dad comes back to pick us up."

I drove a wooden stake into the soft earth at the side of the road using the small sledgehammer provided by Jay's dad while Jay took out his fancy homemade angle measuring device. We'd decided to call this apparatus the Jaytractor, instead of the protractor, because it certainly wasn't PROfessional in design or construction. Jay accused us of teasing him. He was right, and we enjoyed every minute of it.

Jay and I collaborated, using his device to take the angular measurement as best as we could. It was a crude measurement, but we decided, after a vote, on 52°. The next bit of fun involved measuring the baseline; not that the word 'fun' could be connected at all to the process we were going to use. We were a little too democratic, in my opinion, when it was decided by a vote of three to one that I would be the trail man.

Still going my way, I thought, less than pleased.

Since our rope was only 300 feet long, every 300 feet I would get left behind holding the end of the rope. When the rope ran out they would have to stop and wait for me to catch up and then we would have to repeat the process. So I stood there holding the end of the rope, with no one to talk to, while the other three went off up the road, chatting happily away. If anything, it was actually a lot more boring than it seems when you read about it. Fortunately, it was a fairly nice afternoon. Not too hot for an unintended walk down a country road. It had rained a couple of days ago, so even the dust wasn't too bad.

We had agreed that once we got near Georgie's relatives' place we would try to tiptoe by. I had already exceeded my embarrassment quota for the day, and, although in my opinion the others were under quota, they agreed silence was the best policy. We almost got past Georgie's relatives' place unscathed by any embarrassing questions from the sidelines, but just as we'd started to congratulate ourselves on our quiet bypass, two of Georgie's small cousins popped their heads out of the long grass by the side of the road.

"What are you doing back here now? What's going on? Do we need to go and tell your mom you're back?" they asked.

Georgie gave them a couple of our picnic cookies to calm them down and they went back to playing in their imaginary house at the side of the road.

By the time we got down to the next corner we had completed 29 measurements at 300 feet a piece. We were reluctant to go any further but realized that the baseline was probably still too short. We agreed unanimously that it was time for lunch: it's easier to make decisions when you're not hungry.

We decided to have our picnic sitting on some conveniently provided stones from a nearby farmer's field, commonly known as a stone pile. This picnic was the best idea of the day by far. We had chicken sandwiches, nonalcoholic ginger beer, and some cookies. Sylvia had wisely packed ice around the sandwiches when she'd packed the lunch.

As we sat and chatted, we realized that we didn't have a lot of time left. It was already after three and we knew we needed to measure off anywhere from another 10 to 20 lengths of that 300-foot rope.

I took a piece of paper from the back of the booklet we were recording our information in and wrote the numbers 10 to 20 on it in columns. Then, as neatly as we could, we ripped the paper into squares, each square with one of the numbers on it. We folded up the squares and dropped them into my cap. Since Sylvia had prepared the lunch, we gave her the honour of drawing.

"The winner is 14," she proudly announced.

There wasn't much cheering at the result.

We went on down the road, completing our final measurements without much enthusiasm. You can do the math, but you know we measured off more than 12,000 feet. (It was 12,900 feet, actually.) Fortunately, we could still see the tree. Thank heavens there was no significant dip in the road. Jay got out his trusty Jaytractor and we measured the final angle. This angle was roughly 67°. In theory, we now had enough information to determine how far away that tree was.

We were tired, but we were pleased. Our plans hadn't worked out as we'd thought they would, but we'd improvised, and we did have the information we needed. Even better, we still had time to get back to George's relatives before Jay's dad came to pick us up.

It had been quite an afternoon.

Monday, May 14 to
Saturday, May 19

FOR THE NEXT FOUR DAYS, as part of our homework, Jay and I worked on the assignment.

We divided the work up. I did most of the writing. I included a small preamble that included the purpose, method, and list of required equipment. Then I added a section titled 'Summary Comments'. In this section, I outlined the problems we ran into and how we solved them. Jay handled the observations, calculations, and conclusions. He sketched a great map laying out the concession roads, the bush, and our landmark tree and included the measurements – both distance and angles – on it. The calculations page produced the distances to the tree from both endpoints. These distances were the numbers that Mr. Graf was after.

After Thursday night we had our project in great shape, completed and ready to submit, and we celebrated with ginger beer and homemade cookies. Friday afternoon we proudly presented our assignment to Mr. Graf. He was astounded. We were a day early.

This had been a big week for Jay. Earlier in the week, on Tuesday, he'd gotten his driver's license. In his mind, I think getting his license was an accomplishment that even topped our joint completion of the project. Since getting his license, his dad had let him drive the car twice: once to my place on Wednesday, and then again on Thursday night so that we could finish our project.

His dad had become very interested in the project, too. We had talked off and on during the week about going back to the woods on Monday. Monday was only May 21st, but since it was the last Monday before the 24th, it was the official holiday. The Queen's Birthday was my favourite holiday. The weather was usually good and it meant a day off school. My parents even closed the family store; and then, just as dark came, we had our own private fireworks display on that double lot beside our house.

Ever since last Sunday, Jay and I had wanted to return to the woods. Our curiosity had gotten the best of us. We were determined to find that big tree and put a sign on it that said: **Jay and Joel were here**, along with the date. Mr. Jarvis – or Brad, Jay's dad – was almost as curious as we were. He said that he and his wife Carolanne had contacted Jay's uncle Herbert and aunt Emeline. They were going to go for a visit on the holiday Monday. We could go with them. And if we were not too late coming home, Jay could drive us back to Chaseford.

Mr. Jarvis was concerned about us going into that bush. He told us that, according to Herbert, the woods were virtually untouched. Aside from the little bit he owned, nobody had bothered with the bush for years. The neighbouring farmers didn't have much use for it. The bush didn't seem to harbour any animals worth hunting, there was no stream running through it, and there was very dense undergrowth. Once you entered the bush, it was very slow going. It was not a pleasure to walk.

Mr. Jarvis told us that if we were going to go into that bush, we had better decide ahead of time what we needed to take, how we would mark the trail, and set a realistic timeline for returning to the farm. We had to provide him with this information before he would let us go into the bush. That way he knew that we would take it seriously.

I was at the store Saturday afternoon when, once again, Jay appeared to finalize our hiking plan for his dad. Like last time, he arrived about 10 minutes after three, just after my mom had gone home. We decided we would pack our knapsacks with drinks and chocolate bars for a snack and each carry a knife to carve arrows on the trees to mark our trail. We planned to wear long-sleeved shirts turned up around our neck, our socks pulled up over the bottoms of our pants, work boots, and caps. Jay left the store at about four and took our list back to his dad for approval. We wanted to show his dad we were serious. I told Jay I would come over to his house around 7:30 to see what the verdict was. With that, Jay was out the door.

When I got to their door that evening, Jay answered it with his dad standing behind him. His dad gave us the thumbs up sign.

Wow! Mission accomplished!

Monday, May 21

WE WERE BACK AT THE farm again and Jay and I were keen to get started.

"Well boys," said Uncle Herbert, "I hear you have a grand adventure planned. You need to be careful. It's easy to say 'I'm going into the woods and I'll be back in a while', but it's a much more difficult chore than you think. I've only been a short way into that bush myself. After the first 50 yards I started to get confused so I turned around and came back out. I have no more desire to go in there.

"Do you have any idea where you're going? Do you know what direction that tree is?"

"From here in the farmyard, we have a pretty good idea," I said.

Jay took out the map he'd made for our assignment. "This is where we're standing now," he said, pointing at the map. "You can see on the map there's a line of sight that runs across the land not far from where we're standing. That line of sight runs from the first sighting location we used last Sunday to the big tree. We figure that the line of sight intersects the bush about 100 yards from where we are now. So if we follow the edge of the bush for about 100 yards from here, we'll be at the spot where we should enter the bush. Once we enter the bush, we'll do our best to stay pointed in that direction. We're planning to use the sun to keep track of it."

Uncle Herbert roared with laughter. A little too hard, I thought. I think he surprised even himself.

"That's one of the worst plans I've ever heard," he said.

Joel and I were taken aback.

"You boys ever been in a bush before?" he said, chortling. "Once you get in that bush you may never *see* the sun. I hope you have a compass."

Despite our careful planning, our lack of an outdoor education meant we forgot to include a compass in our basic supplies.

"Boys, you can't go into that bush without a compass," said Jay's dad.

It looked like our plans would be on hold. Maybe for a week.

"That's not a problem," said Herbert, speaking up. "I have a compass and it's a good one. Just don't lose it on your journey."

Before he would turn over the compass, Uncle Herbert made us take 15 minutes' worth of practical compass education using the neighbour's barn as a landmark. I guess we passed the test because he said: "I think you'll be okay with that compass." And then he inquired: "Are you going to hold hands when you go in the woods?"

We both showed some obvious discomfort at that question.

"What do you mean?" I stammered.

At that, Herbert and Jay's dad *both* roared with laughter. This seemed to be an afternoon full of fun for them.

"It's okay," Herbert chuckled. "The point is, if you don't have something connecting the two of you, you may easily get separated and lost. That often leads to tragedy in a bush like this. You're going to need a rope that ties the two of you together. I suggest a length of approximately 15 feet."

We looked at him with new respect. We could tell he knew what he was talking about. Joel's dad had been getting pretty nervous about the whole thing, but when he saw we were taking Herbert seriously, he seemed to be okay. Now we were *really* ready to go. Jay and I headed out along the edge of the bush.

"Hold on," said Herbert, stalling us again. "Do either of you know how to use a shotgun?"

Once more, Herbert had surprised us. Jay's uncle was full of surprises.

"I can use a shotgun," I said. "I've been out with my dad shooting a couple of times."

"What do they need a shotgun for?" said Jay's dad. "I don't want them killing game out there. I really don't want them shooting in the bush."

"They won't be able to see any game anyway," said Herbert. "But a shotgun can be a very important safety device. They'll only use it if they get lost or run into a problem. They are absolutely not to shoot that gun under any other circumstance. A shot from that gun is a signal for a search party to set out after them as soon as possible. Two shots in a row mean someone is injured. After the initial shot, they're to fire a shot every 15 minutes. That way, the search party can zero in on them."

Now Uncle Herbert was getting to us. We were getting pretty nervous about the whole darn thing.

Herbert left for a minute and then he came back with the shotgun and a box of shells. I looked at Jay.

"We thought we had a good solid plan," I said. "But your uncle has helped us an awful lot to fill in some pretty important details."

"That's true." Jay turned to his uncle. "Thanks a lot, Uncle Herbert. You're a real expert."

We set off once more along the edge of the bush, and this time the adults let us go. Uncle Herbert was beaming and Jay's dad was smiling. They both hollered goodbye and reminded us to be careful, adding that they had too many women to answer to if anything happened to us. We turned around and waved and then started off into the bush.

THE FIRST 5 YARDS WASN'T too bad; we could still see the farmyard. After another 5 yards, we realized that we were having trouble seeing the edge of the bush, the place where we had entered.

The bush was densely overgrown, full of fallen trees and under-growth. Most of the trees met at the top to form a canopy that in most places let in little light. Gradually, however, our eyes grew accustomed to the dimness. It was so dark that, despite the daylight, the bush seemed menacing. From time to time there were places where the trees weren't packed quite so tight and the visibility momentarily improved, but I was glad it was only two in the afternoon and a clear bright day. I wouldn't have wanted to try this in the dark.

We decided we'd better mark a tree about every 20 feet. We used a knife to make a mark on the reasonable-size trees near the trail, but we also snapped as many small trees along the way as we could. It was very slow going. Jay had previously estimated that we had a little over a mile to go in this direction before we reached the hill that held the big tree, but at the rate we were going, I began to wonder whether we would have enough time to get to the landmark and back to the farmyard on time. Before leaving the farmyard, it had been agreed that we should be back by 4:30 PM at the latest. We kept stumbling along, going as quickly as we dared, and it was about as difficult a thing as I had ever done. We were in the middle of nowhere, heading towards a large tree that we couldn't even see. It was an uncomfortable feeling, almost frightening.

After half an hour, we stopped for a drink and a piece of chocolate bar and to check our bearings. Though we were tired and a little nervous, we didn't want to give up. We realized that this was really quite an adventure and to satisfy ourselves we had to make it to the big tree. We talked about how well planned we'd thought our trip was before uncle Herbert showed us what real planning was about, and about how lucky we were to have had his advice. The break and the sugar gave us some of our spunk back. We would persevere.

It was a real slog. After another 10 minutes, we came across a poorly defined trail. It didn't look like a walking trail. Though Jay's uncle had said there were no animals in the bush, Jay said:

"It looks like a deer trail."

"If it is, it's good news," I said hopefully. "It probably leads some-place a deer wants to go. It may even be someplace we want to go. Somewhere sensible, such as an open space, or to water. Let's follow it for a while, but keep an eye on our compass, too. We'll see whether this trail takes us roughly in the direction we want to go."

So we followed the trail. It was easier going and we made better time. We became a little concerned when, after a few minutes, the trail seemed to be veering away from our target. We decided we would follow the path another five minutes and then check the compass and re-assess whether we were headed in the right direction. At the end of the five minutes, when we rechecked, the path had curved back in the di-rection we wanted to go. Evidently, the deer were smarter than we were.

We'd been walking now for almost an hour and we still hadn't come to any kind of rise in the land. It seemed like an awful long time to spend going a mile; but then, this wasn't easy terrain. It wasn't just the dense growth, either; the land seemed to rise and fall irregularly, and the ups and downs were really noticeable once you were in the bush. But we plodded on, undaunted, and about 10 minutes later Jay stopped and held up his hand.

"I think we're starting to go uphill," he said.

"Look ahead to the right," I said as we soldiered on. "I know you can't see very far, but doesn't it look a little brighter?"

We set off towards that brighter area. The land continued to rise and within another five minutes we were breaking into a clearing.

Hallelujah!

We ran and jumped around that open glade like little kids at Christmas. We'd made it! We were on the hill and the big tree was only 50 yards away!

We were really excited. After all that worrying about not knowing where we were, and the fear we'd had about going in the wrong direc-tion, we felt elated. That forest that had given us a real dose of fear!

"So far, so good," said Jay. He reached into his knapsack and pulled out a little wooden sign. "It's time to decorate the tree. After all, it does feel a little bit like Christmas."

We went over to the tree and attached the sign to it using the hammer and nails we'd brought with us.

Jay and Joel were here, Monday May 21, 1928, the sign proclaimed.

"I don't see any other signs on this tree," said Joel, standing back and looking it over, "so I guess we can claim it as ours."

"I think maybe we should just leave the tree here in the bush for now," I said, chuckling.

"That wasn't remotely funny," said Jay, giving me a look.

We sat down, leaned our backs against our landmark tree, and took another refreshment break.

"I'd like to get up in the tree and look around a bit," I said after a couple of minutes. "I know there's not much to see but bush, but since we're here."

"I don't know how you're going to get up in this tree," said Joel, squinting up at it. "It's a big tree and there aren't many lower limbs we can reach."

"It's not as big a problem as you think, Jay," I answered confidently. "See the tree beside it? It's big enough that we can climb it and then transfer over to the large tree."

We put our knapsacks on the ground, as well as the shotgun and our flashlights, then climbed the smaller tree and scrambled over to the big tree. We climbed up to a branch that was large enough to support our weight and high enough to give us a reasonable view of the surroundings. With the help of the hill, we were now up high enough to see past a lot of the neighbouring trees.

We quickly noted that, when we looked back in the direction from which we'd come, we could see nothing but bush. We weren't far enough up the tree to see back to the farmyard, or even to the rise of the neighbouring road where we'd staked out our baseline the Sunday before. So we looked in the other direction.

"Holy Toledo!" Jay yelled, pointing excitedly.

I looked in the direction Jay was pointing. It took me a moment to figure out what he'd seen, but then I yelled, too: just a couple hundred yards away we could see – just barely – the top of what appeared to be a shack. We couldn't believe our eyes.

"I think we've seen the impossible," I said. "Your uncle Herbert will be very surprised. He told us nobody's been in these woods for years. Why would there be a shack way back here where nobody could get to it? Who would put it here? What would they use it for? This just doesn't make any sense."

From where we were, we couldn't see any signs of anybody having been in the area for a long time.

"I don't care whether it makes sense or not," said Jay. "It's part of our adventure today. We'd better go over and take a closer look at that shack."

We descended the tree safely, put on our knapsacks, and grabbed our flashlights. I picked up the shotgun and we headed towards the shack.

It was fairly easygoing to get there. A lot easier than the first part of our journey. The trees seemed to thin out as we moved towards the shack, and as we got closer we noticed that a little bit of the brush had been cleared away from around the cabin. Some of the longer grass and brush had been tramped down a bit, probably by horses, so we decided to be cautious.

We got as close to the shack as we could without being easily spotted and then agreed to wait for about 10 minutes to listen and look around carefully before proceeding. The cabin was not large. It looked to be only about 12 feet by 15 feet. It was about 3:15 PM, so if we were going to look, now was the time. We had just enough time for a quick look inside. We'd have to start back soon if we were going to meet the 4:30 PM deadline.

Nothing seemed amiss, so, feeling brave, we approached the shack.

It wasn't fancy. There were two windows: one at the front, and one on what I supposed was the east side. We couldn't look through the windows, though, because they'd been battened down from inside. Primarily, I supposed, to keep out any friendly wildlife. The only easy way to see inside was to open the door.

There was a hole in the door about 2 ½ feet from the bottom edge, about the size of a penny. Some twine ran through the hole, made a loop, and hooked over a nail that had been hammered into the outside wall about 2 inches from the door.

"Looks like an old-fashioned door latch," said Jay.

"Inexpensive but effective," I replied.

I unhooked the twine and Jay nudged the door open with his foot.

The moment he'd done so, we wished we'd left the door closed. The smell was overpowering. With the door closed, the smell had been trapped inside, waiting for us.

We both turned and threw up. Then, when we'd recovered, we put our hands over our noses and entered. We couldn't have walked away from that cabin at that moment if we'd wanted to; something compelled us to go in. When our eyes adjusted to the light, we saw a body on the floor. It looked like a woman. I didn't want to cry, but I was so overwhelmed it was hard not to.

Jay and I quickly went back outside, shaking and gagging. I picked up the shotgun, loaded a shell, pointed the gun up at the sky, and pulled the trigger. There was a loud, explosive bang but we hardly noticed.

"Take a look at your watch," said Jay. "You shoot again in 15 minutes."

JAY'S PARENTS, BRAD and Carolanne, were sitting on the front porch of the farmhouse with Herbert and Emeline, having a pleasant chitchat. Emeline had baked some butter tarts the previous evening, and the tarts, along with the tea and conversation, were making for a nice afternoon in the country.

Carolanne and Herbert were brother and sister, so there was some talk about that family: the usual topics, like who is getting married, who had died, who had been born, and who was having marital trouble. Those topics, although very interesting, were finally depleted, and they moved onto what construction projects Brad had lined up for the summer. The next subject on the agenda was the boys and their project. As if on cue, there was a distant bang. It was not loud, but everybody stopped and looked at each other.

"Herbert, is that what I think it is?" said Brad.

"Yes, that sounds like the shotgun," said Herbert.

The women looked at each other, obviously upset.

"What does it mean?" said Carolanne.

"It means the boys have run into a problem," said Brad. "That shot was a signal. It means we should mount a search party to go out and see what's happened to them. They could be lost, or they could have encountered some other problem. We know they aren't injured, at least."

"How do you know that?" both women asked almost simultaneously, worried expressions on their faces.

"We only heard one shot," said Herbert. "For an injury, they were to fire two shots. There's no point imagining it to be a worse situation than it might be. Brad and I will put on our walking boots, grab our flashlights, and grab a couple of shotguns. We'll take that stretcher I've got stored in that shed area attached to the back of the summer kitchen, too, just in case. It's been waiting there for an emergency. I don't think we'll need it, but we'll take it anyway. You two ladies need to stay right here. It's about 3:45 right now. Give us two hours. That should give us enough time to get there and back, especially if the boys blazed a good trail. If we're not back by 5:45, then you need to contact the law in Chaseford."

With that, Herbert went into the house, got his walking boots, a couple of shotguns, and a couple of flashlights. Brad went to the car, rummaged around for his walking boots, and put them on. Herbert also brought out a couple of long-sleeved shirts and gave one to Brad. It was a little small on Brad, but it was better than not having your arms covered in the bush. There were lots of hungry mosquitoes and black flies in that bush waiting for supper. The two men put their hats on, waved goodbye, and set off down the trail that Joel and Jay had marked out just a couple of hours earlier.

It wasn't easy going, but the boys had done a good job marking the trail. About 10 minutes into their foray, Brad and Herbert heard another gunshot.

"Looks like the boys followed your advice," said Brad. "That was a good plan."

Herbert smiled and they both continued down the trail.

They pushed forward through the undergrowth until they reached the deer trail and there Herbert and Brad were momentarily stumped. Then they noticed that a yard or so up the trail a tree had been marked by one of the boys with a knife.

"They must have used this deer trail," said Brad.

They were only on the deer trail a couple of minutes when they heard a third shot. Just a few minutes later, they noticed the ground rising and could see that the bush was thinning.

As they came out of the bush, they spotted the big tree. They approached the tree and read the sign that Jay and Joel had posted.

Brad smiled faintly at Herbert and said: "We know they got this far, anyway. But where the heck are they now?"

Brad and Herbert were concerned. They had arrived at the tree but there was no sign of the boys.

They walked around the edge of the clearing looking for any signs that would show them which way the boys had headed. They didn't have any luck finding the next part of the trail, so they decided to sit and rest. They'd had an easier time than Jay and Joel following the trail through the bush, but it had still demanded a lot of exercise, along with the odd curse. The men figured that if they waited for the next gunshot it would help them determine which direction to go. They were chatting only a couple of minutes when they heard a gunshot not very far away. They got up and headed down the other side of the hill in the direction the shot had come from. The bush had thinned out a lot here, making travel much easier, and within five minutes they burst into an open area. At about the same time they saw both the boys and the cabin behind them. The two boys hurried over to them, their faces pale. They didn't look well, but neither boy seemed to be injured.

"What in heaven's name is the problem?" Brad exclaimed. "It wasn't an easy trip out here."

Jay grimaced and seemed to be on the verge of tears. "There's a body in the cabin," he blurted.

Everybody went quickly to the cabin. Joel and Jay waited outside while Jay's dad and Uncle Herbert entered. They were only in there a few seconds before they came back out and promptly, and in an undignified manner, emptied their stomachs.

"That's a terrible stench in there," Uncle Herbert said, coughing. "We need to call the police. We have to head back to the farmhouse. Right now."

The return trip through the bush was much quicker. Now that much of the undergrowth along the way had been tramped down a bit, you could almost see a trail. It still wasn't easy going, but what was missing was the fear of not knowing where you were going or what you might find when you got there. Still, they couldn't shake the sense of dread they felt about finding that body in the cabin. Had the person died there of natural causes or was it something more sinister? They didn't know. But they did know that they had to get the law involved.

The trip back only took them about 25 minutes. They arrived at the farmhouse just after 5:30 PM, and ahead of their deadline, but even so they could see that Emeline and Carolanne had been fretting the whole time they'd been gone. When all four of them walked out of the bush under their own steam, there was a noticeable look of relief on the faces of both women. Until that moment, they'd been sure someone had been badly injured and were very happy to see that everyone had come back in one piece. But those smiles and happy glances disappeared when they found out what the boys had discovered.

"We need to phone the police right now," said Herbert, heading into the house.

"It's a holiday, Herbert," Emeline hollered after him. "You'll have to be patient."

They'd had a telephone on the farm for a couple of years now. Emeline had recently read in the local newspaper that there were now one million telephones in the Dominion of Canada. That worked out to one telephone for every 10 people, and they were still not to be found in many farmhouses. They were on a party line, so Herbert knew that by the time he contacted the police there would be other interested parties in the neighbourhood. Not everyone respected your privacy on the party line.

Herbert had to phone to Chaseford because it was the closest municipality with a police force. Chaseford had a chief of police, a sergeant, and three constables. Today was holiday Monday and Herbert knew that it might take more than one call to locate the chief of police. As it turned out, the chief, Bob Petrovic, was at home. He and his family were having a family dinner to celebrate his mother's 75th birthday.

Herbert gave the chief a brief outline of what had happened. The chief, who had about 25 years of police experience, had seen bodies before and he responded quickly.

"I'll be out there within the hour, with my constable, Jake Smith," he said.

The chief told Herbert that he planned to go to the cabin that evening. At this time of year, there was still quite a bit of light until at least 8:30 PM. They would just have to sit tight until then.

Herbert went back to the porch and brought everybody up to date. Emeline immediately got up and went to the kitchen. With Carolanne's help, they rummaged around in the kitchen and prepared a quick supper. After their trek through the bush, the men were hungry. They figured they had about an hour to eat and rest before the chief arrived.

THE LOCAL POLICE HAD two vehicles: a new Ford Radio Motor Patrol car, and a Studebaker police paddy wagon. The local town council had, over the last few years, been reluctant to make these purchases; but once they had, the mayor of Chaseford was always proud, on any occasion, to proclaim they had an up-to-date police force with up-to-date vehicles. So, as we all sat down to supper, we expected to see the chief and Cst. Smith pull into the farmyard in the patrol car.

The supper was good: mashed potatoes and roast beef left over from Sunday's supper, along with some fresh vegetables right out of the garden. Of course, we had apple pie for dessert. Nobody makes it better than Emeline. With the meal over, and without a democratic election, Jay and I were selected for KP duty while everyone else went out to relax on the porch and await the two policemen. Emeline had left a full kettle of water heating on the stove, so as soon as we had the table cleared off and things returned either to the icebox or the cupboards, the hot water was ready for dishes.

About 10 minutes after Jay and I finished the dishes, the chief of police and Cst. Smith arrived. The two policemen got out of the car and joined us on the porch. No introductions were necessary; everyone was previously acquainted.

"We don't have a lot of time before dark," said the chief. "So you'd better tell me what happened again. Then take us to the body."

Jay and I told the chief about finding the cabin in the woods and then finding a body in the cabin.

"Why did you go in the woods?" said the chief. He seemed perplexed by this. "I've never heard of anybody going into this bush. What was the motivation?"

Jay and I explained our trigonometry assignment and the chief said: "You sure picked a humdinger of a landmark."

The chief told us he might have more questions for us later, but that we would have to get going since it was already 7:15. There was not a lot of daylight left.

This time we brought a couple of lanterns with us as well. They would be more effective than the flashlights if dark came before we were ready for it. We got through the bush pretty fast this time, and after 20 minutes of following a now well-trod path, we arrived at the big tree. In another five minutes, we were down the hill and standing in front of the cabin. We stood back and let the chief and the constable enter. They were quickly back outside.

Though they'd covered their noses with their handkerchiefs before entering, the chief exclaimed loudly: "That was a hell of a smell!"

"It's almost as bad as the time we found Mark Peters dead in that room he rented above the barbershop," said Cst. Smith. "Remember that, Chief? He'd been closed up in there for about a week in the summer. I still think that was the worst."

"Jake, as my constable, you now have the unpleasant duty of going back into the cabin," said the chief. "Prop those inside window coverings up. We need to get a little fresh air in there."

"Do we need a stretcher?" said Herbert. "Brad and I brought one with us when we came looking for the boys. It's still here."

"We're not going to touch the body," said the chief, shaking his head. "The coroner will have to come out here tomorrow. He'll likely have help and a stretcher with him. You might as well take yours back with you tonight. I think we're done here, except for Jake. Sorry Jake, but you've been elected. Someone has to stay here to protect the body. There's screening in the windows, so I don't think animals are going to get in there easily."

"I wasn't planning on a sleepover," said Cst. Smith, grimacing. "That floor will be awfully hard."

"I have a sleeping bag he can use," said Herbert.

"I think we should all head back to the farm now," said the chief. "The body will be okay until Jake gets back with the sleeping bag."

We arrived back at the farmhouse just as the sun was setting. Herbert got the sleeping bag for Jake, and the constable, with lantern and sleeping bag in hand, got ready to head back to the cabin. It wasn't a trip I would have wanted to make, but Cst. Smith didn't seem worried about it.

"I have a light and my gun and overtime pay headed my way," said the constable. "If I take my time, I'll be okay." And with that, he departed.

For Jay and me, it had been an incredible day. But it was not a day we wanted to repeat and we were glad it was finally over.

Tuesday, May 22

DR. FRANK WHITTLES, the coroner, arrived at Herbert and Emeline's farm shortly before 8 o'clock Tuesday morning. He brought his assistant Bobby Degood with him.

The Coroner asked Emeline if he could speak to Herbert as soon as possible. She told him Herbert was in the barn, feeding the cattle, and Dr. Whittles headed that way.

As soon as he entered the barn, Herbert hollered at him.

"Hello, Frank! What's the local coroner doing in my barn?" Herbert and Frank had been friends for many years, so with a big smile, Herbert added: "You're just the guy I need. I've got lots of chores to do today."

Frank returned the smile. "At your earliest convenience, I need you to put me and my assistant on the right path to the cabin," he said.

"I'll do that right now," said Herbert. "We're only about two minutes from the start of the trail."

Dr. Whittles and Bobby Degood followed Herbert to the start of the trail. By this point, the trail was well beaten down and the coroner and his assistant could find their way on their own. It was only a 20-minute walk to the hill with the big tree and when they arrived they noticed a crude sign posted on a nearby tree indicating with an arrow and the word "**cabin**" what direction to follow next. Just as they arrived in the clearing, the cabin door opened and Cst. Smith stepped out.

"Good morning," Cst. Smith said with enthusiasm. "I was getting tired of being here alone. The only company I had wasn't very talkative. Did you see the signpost I put up this morning?"

"The sign was legible, Jake, but you're going to have to work on your craftsmanship," said Dr. Whittles. "Now show me the victim."

Cst. Smith led the coroner and Bobby Degood into the cabin.

"It's still pretty smelly in here, Jake," said Bobby.

"You should've been here last night," said Cst. Smith. "I've had all the window shutters open since about 8 o'clock last evening. It's hardly noticeable now."

"Has anybody touched this body?" Dr. Whittles interrupted.

"I don't believe so," said Cst. Smith. "The chief and I didn't touch it, and from what we've been told nobody else has touched it since it was found yesterday afternoon."

"Get your notepad and pencil ready Bobby," said Dr. Whittles. "Let's take a look."

The coroner bent down close to the body. The body was face down on the cabin floor. Before turning the body, he examined the clothing, looking for blood or any tears in the material.

"There appear to be no wounds on the victim's back, and the clothes don't appear to have been tampered with in any way," he announced.

Bobby carefully noted this information on his pad.

"Okay, Bobby. You help me and we'll turn her over."

"It's a woman?" said Bobby.

"Apparently so. Most men don't wear fancy riding outfits like this," said Dr. Whittles.

He turned to Cst. Smith.

"Did you see any sign of a horse around here? Or any place a horse may have been tied up?"

"I haven't had a chance to look yet," said Cst. Smith. "The thought never crossed my mind."

"Would you mind taking a look around the perimeter of the clearing to see if there's any sign that a horse has been here?" said Dr. Whittles.

"Not a problem," said Cst. Smith. And away he went.

"Bobby, please note that there is a significant wound to the right side of her temple," said Dr. Whittles. "There don't appear to be any other external signs of trauma to the body. Also note that the body is not totally cold yet. But I don't think there's any point in using a thermometer to measure the body temperature. According to what I've read, the body temperature drops about 2 ¾ degrees Fahrenheit for every hour the victim has been dead. We know she had been dead some time prior to the boys finding the body. That was at or about 3 o'clock yesterday afternoon. That's already more than 18 hours ago. According to the boys, there was a significant odour at the time of discovery, so she had been dead some time prior to that. Also, there is no rigor mortis remaining in the body. That means, again, she's been dead more than 18 hours. So I don't think I'm going to be able to place her time of death with much accuracy. But my experience tells me that she died probably not much more than a day prior to the time that the boys found the body."

Bobby made another note on his pad.

"We'll have to take the body back to town," the coroner continued. "We can do a proper autopsy on her once the next of kin has been notified. But before we move the body we need to take a look around the area where she fell to see if there are any other clues. I didn't bring the fingerprint kit with us today. That's on tomorrow's agenda. We do need to check the area close to the body to see whether there's anything at all of interest. Once we have her on the stretcher and out of the cabin, we'll take another look on the floor where the body has been lying."

After they completed their search of the surrounding floor area in the cabin, Dr. Whittles and Bobby very carefully lifted the body onto the stretcher. Then they carried the stretcher through the cabin door and placed it down very carefully in a grassy area just outside the door.

"While we're here, Bobby, we're going to do a little inventory," said Dr. Whittles. "So get your notepad out."

Their inventory included a small table, two wooden chairs, and a small cupboard.

"There's not much in here," Dr. Whittles said. "This place is suspiciously empty. I have the feeling that maybe somebody tidied things up. For an old cabin that nobody knew about, it's pretty clean and in decent repair. Those wooden shutters appear to have been used regularly." He sighed. "Okay, Bobby, let's leave the rest of this to the detectives."

Just then Cst. Smith returned.

"Guess what?" he said, pointing. "About 100 feet from here, down where you see that clump three or four trees, there's a tying post for horses. There's also evidence that horses have been here before. Not far from there I also found what looks like a small dumpsite. There's nothing really fresh there and it looks like someone has had at least one fire to burn a lot of it. I investigated further and found a place behind the cabin where someone's been doing some cooking. It looks like they've dug a bit of a pit and put stones around it to keep the fire contained. It seems like the victim, and perhaps other people, have been here before. This cabin, that seems to be in such an isolated place, is not unknown to some people. A great place to have some solitude or to have a private meeting. Also, just past where I saw the tie-up for the horse, there appears to be a trail that leads away from here opposite from the direction we came from. The bush doesn't seem to be near as thick in that direction."

"The Chief is going to be really pleased by your initiative, Jake," said Dr. Whittles. "And I'm going to be really pleased after you help us get this body back to the farmyard."

"The Chief said I was supposed to guard the site," said Cst. Smith.

"Good try, Jake," said the coroner, "but you know that when the body's gone you don't need to guard the site. The Chief told me you're to come back to town with Bobby and myself."

"Oh well, I tried," said Cst. Smith, smiling. "I suppose I have to help Bobby haul that body back through the bush?"

"You are correct," Dr. Whittles said with a grin. "Look on the bright side: think of all the exercise and fresh air."

"I hope there's a good meal in it for me somewhere soon," said Cst. Smith.

"As soon as we get back to town I'll take you to Mabel's Diner," said Dr. Whittles. "You know she serves the best big breakfast in town. We might get there a little late, but I know she'll cook something up for a valuable policeman like yourself. The treat will be on the town of Chaseford."

With that vision in mind, Cst. Smith said: "Then let's get this show on the road!"

The four of them – three living, one dead – headed down the trail back to Herbert and Emeline's farm.

THAT SAME DAY AT SCHOOL there were quite a few rumours going around. There had been more excitement than usual on the Victoria Day holiday. I don't think anybody else really knew much about what had happened, but with that party line, everybody knew the chief of police and his sidekick Jake had been out to Herbert and Emeline's farm. They just didn't know any of the details.

Trigonometry was our last class of the day, and when Jay and I entered, Mr. Graf smiled at us, leaving us momentarily puzzled.

"I will now collect those assignments that are due today," he said. "You will be penalized with a late penalty if you're not able to hand in your assignment by the end of class. I think I am being reasonable. I would like to point out to you that *some* assignments were handed in as early as last Friday. So you have no excuse."

We now understood Mr. Graf's smile: we were the golden boys. At least for today. Hopefully no one else would find out who had handed in their assignments early.

When the school day ended, it didn't take long for Georgie and Sylvia to catch up with us. They were really looking forward to that walk home. They said they needed and deserved an update. And I guess they did. They had taken part in the first half of our adventure. And Sylvia had been the one who'd suggested the tree as a landmark. So we told them the whole story. We even told them about the body and that the coroner was supposed to be out there today.

"Beyond that, we don't know anything," I said.

I guess that was pretty exciting information for the girls. I knew they were going to pick up some additional points at home after talking to their moms and dads about these developments. This was about the biggest thing to hit Chaseford since that tragic car accident last year that killed two young people.

Wednesday, May 23

DR. WHITTLES, THE CORONER, was anxious to do the autopsy. He was hoping to perform it on Wednesday, but Wednesday morning had arrived and the body still hadn't been identified. As the next of kin had not yet been notified, he did not have permission to perform the autopsy. The body would have to be kept on ice until the victim's family could be located.

Based on his visual examination, Dr. Whittles had determined that the head wound was not significant and was not likely a contributing factor to death. A woman dying alone in a remote cabin, no matter the cause, seemed to be very suspicious.

THE CHIEF OF POLICE had been busy as well. He had made another trip out to the cabin and his return visit had left him baffled. No further clues had been found. He still wasn't convinced that the cabin was the scene of a crime. In Chaseford and area, if they had a murder, it was usually a crime of passion. It wasn't too complicated to figure out what had happened if a shooting or stabbing, or even strangulation, was involved.

Upon his return to town, Chief Petrovic visited the coroner. Dr. Whittles informed him that, from his brief visual examination, he had doubts that it was a simple accident, or that the woman had died from natural causes. He asked the chief of police if he had had any luck identifying the body and finding the next of kin.

"Not yet," said the chief. "I guess your autopsy will have to wait. After listening to your opinion, Frank, I'm more inclined to think she may have met with foul play. I think we need the help of a bona fide detective experienced in murder investigations."

The chief of police talked to the mayor next. He told the mayor that he and the coroner had been discussing a body found in a cabin last Sunday. The chief described it as a suspicious death and asked for permission to consult with the police force in London. He told the mayor they needed to involve a detective experienced in the investigation of homicides. The mayor agreed. London was a city with a full-fledged police force with several departments and it had several respected detectives.

After contacting the London police, the chief reported back to the mayor that they'd agreed to send him Det. Gerald O'Neill. Det. O'Neill would be arriving Thursday afternoon and would be available until the end of June, working on the case as needed. On days he wasn't required in Chaseford, he was to report to the London police station for assignment. Until Det. O'Neill arrived, it was important for the chief of police to secure the crime scene, so it looked like Cst. Smith would be enjoying another campout in the woods. Something the police chief knew the constable would be eager to participate in.

THE CHIEF AND DET. Gerald O'Neill left Chaseford for the cabin about 2:30 Thursday afternoon. On the trip out to the cabin, the chief brought Det. O'Neill up to date, telling him as much as he could remember. He even mentioned Jay and Joel's school project. Det. O'Neill asked Chief Petrovic what he knew about the identity of the victim. The chief said there was nothing on the woman's body to identify her, but the coroner placed her somewhere in her early 50s. The chief said he had one of his constables over at the county office attempting to trace the ownership of the land that the cabin sat on.

The chief and Det. O'Neill made a brief stop at Herbert and Emeline's farm for introductions. The chief told them he appreciated their cooperation and hoped that their routine wouldn't be too disrupted over the next few weeks. He said that the second trail, the one leading to the cabin from the side road on the other edge of the bush, would be checked thoroughly today. Since the bush in that direction appeared not to be as dense, that was the trail they would likely be using most of the time in the future. Then the two policemen left and headed up the trail.

When they arrived at the cabin, the chief introduced Det. O'Neill to Cst. Smith. Cst. Smith quickly determined that Det. O'Neill was a friendly fellow and someone who didn't miss much.

"Okay," said the detective. "Take me on the tour, Jake. Let's start with the cabin, then take a look at that cooking site. Next, we'll look at the area where the horses were tied up. Then we'll take a trip down the other trail to the next side road. By then, we'll both be ready for supper." Det. O'Neill turned to the chief. "When Jake and I head down the unexplored trail, would you be kind enough to drive around to the next concession and wait for us?"

"I can do that," said Chief Petrovic. "I had Jake scout out that trail yesterday. He followed it down to the next concession road. He said it's a little over a mile and the bush goes pretty much to the road. On the other side of the road the land is fairly open. There's very little bush. Jake put a **Stay Out** sign at the entrance to the trail."

"Okay, let's head to the cabin," said Det. O'Neill.

Once they were in the cabin, the detective asked about the head wound the victim had received.

"According to the coroner, it doesn't look like the woman was struck with a heavy blunt object," said the chief. "It looks more like she hit her head as she fell. The coroner doesn't think it's from hitting the floor."

"Looking at the chalk outline showing where the body was located, and where the furniture's currently located, I don't see what she hit her head on," said Det. O'Neill. "Let's see if something was moved."

"Wow," said Cst. Smith. "That's a great idea." He was already impressed with the London detective.

They got down on their hands and knees, examining the floor. Close scrutiny revealed that the small cupboard had been moved. Jake and the chief moved the cupboard back to what appeared to be its original position. That uncovered a stain on the floor where the cupboard had been sitting. When they got close to the stain, they noticed no odour, and the area was dry. Further examination of the cabin revealed no additional clues.

They found nothing at the cooking site. The dumpsite yielded very little as well. They now found themselves at the spot where the horse or horses had been tied up.

After closely examining the area near the tie-up post, Det. O'Neill said: "From the size of the area of grass that has recently been tramped down – that's within the last week or so – I suspect more than one horse was tied up here. If you look closely, you'll also notice there are two different sizes of horseshoes in evidence. Either one horse was somewhat smaller than the other, or it's not the same breed." Det. O'Neill straightened up. "Okay, Jake, let's head down the trail. We'll meet you at the next side road, Chief."

"You'll likely beat me," said Chief Petrovic. "I have to walk the trail back to my car."

After they parted company, the detective turned to Jake.

"It'll take us a little time to do the trail. I'm going to take a look at the first four or five feet to the right of the trail while you take a look the same distance from the left side of the trail. Who knows what we may find."

The first 10 minutes were uneventful. Then Cst. Smith saw something shiny just a couple of feet further off the trail than he had been looking.

"Wait a minute. Gerald, come over here. I think I found something. It looks like a tin cup."

"Don't touch a thing," said the detective. "If we're lucky we'll find fingerprints."

The two of them got down and did a thorough search of the nearby area and found another cup and an empty whisky bottle. They carefully put their prizes in Cst. Smith's knapsack, pleased with their find. The journey down the rest of the trail was uneventful. When he arrived at the road, the chief was there.

"Well boys," said the chief, "either I'm really fast or it took you a bit longer than I thought it would."

"Gerald and I examined both sides of the trail and came up with some prizes," said Cst. Smith.

"It's a little after six and I'm hungry," said the chief. "Let's go to Mabel's Diner, have today's special, and a chinwag."

Friday, May 25

ON FRIDAY MORNING, Det. O'Neill, the chief of police, and Cst. Smith took one more thorough look at what they now thought was the scene of a crime. They didn't turn up any more clues, however, so they returned to town for lunch.

Det. O'Neill said he'd return on Monday and hoped that they'd be able to start at 9 o'clock in the morning with a meeting at the office of the chief of police. At their Monday morning meeting, he wanted to make a list of the people they would interview and the questions they would ask. They'd start by interviewing the farmers living in the area. He said he understood that it would be a little difficult, because at this point in time nobody knew who owned the property, but he'd be back with a list of suggested interview questions. Aside from the local landowners, their list of interviewees would include Herbert and Emeline Derrigan, Joel Franklin and his parents, Jay Smith and his parents, and anybody else who had been involved in the business from the start. Sometimes, he explained, the slightest bit of information, no matter how irrelevant it seemed at the time, led to an idea or to another line of questioning that could be helpful.

SHORTLY AFTER LUNCH, Cst. Herman called the chief of police from the registry office.

"I have some news for you, Chief," said Cst. Herman. "But don't get too excited. One of the registry clerks has been searching the title of the land the bush is on. It hasn't been easy to come up with the name of the property owner, but thanks to her help, we have it. The owner's name is 'Bushland Farm.'"

"Thanks a lot, Cst. Herman," said the chief, "but I'll need a lot more help than that. Get back to work and call me when you have some real information."

"Your chief sounds kinda grumpy," said the registry clerk.

Cst. Herman, who was a shade pinker than he had been before the call, agreed.

"I think you should head over to the municipal office, Cst. Herman," said the registry clerk. "They send out the tax bills for Chaseford and the surrounding area from there. If you don't get a name from the tax bill, you'll at least have the address where the tax bill is sent. Just keep in mind that Bushland Farm could be a group of owners, or a family that just decided, on the advice of their accountant, to use the name for business purposes. It does seem somewhat mysterious, though, given that all the other farm property in that area is owned and registered to individual farmers. But this is a very big chunk of land. If you include the 200 acres across from the bush, it's about 4000 acres, though some of the outlying edges of the bush belong to other farmers. You've already met Herbert and Emeline Derrigan, who own about 150 acres of that bush in addition to their farmland."

"That's right," said Cst. Herman. "This whole thing started when Jay Smith and Joel Franklin went to the Derrigan farm to use that big tree as a landmark for their class project."

With these remarks in his mind, Cst. Herman thanked the registry clerk for her help and headed to the municipal office.

At the town office, Cst. Herman spoke to the municipal clerk in charge of tax notices and tax collection, whom he already knew.

"Well, Stan," he said, "you've been doing this job for a number of years. I think I remember coming here once with my parents when they paid their taxes."

"Yes, Peter, your parents were always good customers. They always paid, and paid on time."

"I got a tricky one for you, Stan," said the constable. "I just came from the registry office. I'm trying to track down the owner of some bush land out near Goshawk. The land is in the name of a registered company called Bushland Farm. Unfortunately, we're investigating what we think could be a crime and that doesn't help us. We need to get a real name. I know you'll have the address where you send the tax bill, but I wondered if, maybe in the course of years, you'd ever met anyone who'd come in to pay the bill? Or, since you know almost everybody in the area, I was wondering if you might know the name of the person or persons or family connected to Bushland Farms."

"It's been a long time, Peter, since I've seen anybody with any connection to Bushland Farms," said Stan. "I do recognize the name, though, and up until a few years ago Hugh Carter would come in and pay the tax bill for the property."

"I've never heard of Hugh Carter," said Cst. Herman.

"That's likely because he was before your time, Peter," said Stan, smiling. "At one time, he was a very important man in this area. A person most of us liked and respected. We even voted him to become a Member of Parliament."

"Oh, *that* Hugh Carter," said the constable. "There's a picture of him in the municipal building, not far from the police chief's office. Do you know where he lives?"

"He probably went to heaven," said Stan. "He's been dead at least 15 years. The entire family moved to the Ottawa area shortly after his death. I believe his wife, Ruth, is still alive, however. And he had two sons, Proctor and Amos, and a daughter, Louise. According to my wife, the daughter lives with her mother."

Cst. Herman was pleased with this information and was now looking forward to contacting the chief. He finally had some specific information they could use to further their investigation.

When the chief received the good news from the constable, he said: "Good work, Peter. We'll keep you on staff after all."

Cst. Herman wished he could be entirely certain the chief was kidding.

"I'll get a hold of the Ottawa police department right now," said the chief, "and have them speak to Ruth Carter."

BY THE TIME CHIEF PETROVIC was able to speak to someone in authority at the Ottawa police department, it was 4:30 in the afternoon.

The Chaseford chief of police was put through to the officer in charge of criminal investigations for the Ottawa region, Assistant Chief Dick Rutherford. Chief Petrovic explained to Assistant Chief Rutherford that a mysterious death had occurred on a property just outside of Chaseford. Almost a week had elapsed since the body had been discovered and as of yet they hadn't been able to identify it. Part of the reason for the delay, he explained, was the difficulty they'd had determining the owner of the property that the body had been discovered on, a mystery that had been solved just earlier that morning with the help of the local registry office. The municipal tax officer, Chief Petrovic concluded, had determined that the property owner was the Hugh Carter family.

"Is that the Hugh Carter who was a Member of Parliament?" said Assistant Chief Rutherford when the chief had finished.

"Yes," said Chief Petrovic.

"He was well-respected here in Ottawa. I met him on a couple of official occasions and he was a knowledgeable man," said Rutherford. "He wasn't the least bit arrogant and had great respect for the public. He was always trying to do the right thing. I was sorry when he passed away. Parliament lost a valuable member."

"We're falling behind in this investigation," said Chief Petrovic, seeing his opening. "Would it be possible for you to contact Ruth Carter, Hughes wife? I believe she's still alive and capable. It would be very helpful if a member of the family could come to Chaseford for an interview. They probably have information about the property and the cabin that would be helpful in the investigation."

"I'll see what I can do," said Assistant Chief Rutherford. "If Mrs. Carter, or one of her family, is unable or unwilling to travel to Chaseford you may have to come to Ottawa to conduct your interview."

"Understood."

Chief Petrovic thanked him and their conversation ended.

BECAUSE THIS WAS AN active investigation, and potentially a murder, when Assistant Chief Rutherford finished speaking with the Chaseford Chief of Police, he decided that he would pay Ruth Carter a visit himself.

He had one of his staff find her phone number and address, and, though it was almost 5 o'clock on a Friday afternoon, because of the nature of the investigation, he decided to call anyway.

A person by the name of Bella answered the phone. Rutherford asked Bella if he could speak to Mrs. Carter. She asked who was phoning and there was a brief delay; then Bella informed him that Mrs. Carter would be with him in a moment.

When Mrs. Carter came on the line, Rutherford asked if it was possible for him to visit her sometime on Saturday. She asked him why he wanted to visit and the assistant chief explained that it was about a property they owned in the Chaseford area. Mrs. Carter said she would be pleased to see him at 2:00 PM Saturday and gave him directions to her home.

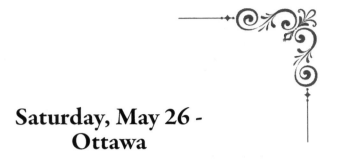

Saturday, May 26 -
Ottawa

WHEN ASSISTANT CHIEF Rutherford arrived at the Carter home he was greeted at the door by a woman in a nurse's uniform. She introduced herself as Bella Frankel.

"Chief Rutherford, I presume? Please come with me. Mrs. Carter will receive you in the living room."

Rutherford did not correct Bella, momentarily enjoying the promotion. A woman, who appeared to be about 80 years of age, was waiting for him in the living room. She was well dressed but seated in a wheelchair. The woman invited him to sit for a cup of tea and Bella left them alone.

Mrs. Carter pointed to a seat across from her and Rutherford seated himself. A small table stood between them with two teacups, a teapot, and a tray of what smelled to be freshly-baked cookies on top.

"I'm happy to have company today, but I'm a little shorthanded," she said. "My daughter Louise usually plays the host. But Bella is extremely capable."

"Thank you for allowing me to visit you on a Saturday," said Rutherford. "I'm sorry you're shorthanded, but I have to say these cookies look and smell wonderful."

Mrs. Carter explained that her daughter Louise lived with her, and that, while they had some outside help from time to time, with Bella's help, they managed quite well. She mentioned also that Bella, her nurse, now lived with them too. Bella had been hired about a year ago, after Mrs. Carter had had her stroke. She went on to say that her daughter Louise had gone back to visit her old stomping grounds in Chaseford.

"Louise hasn't returned yet," Mrs. Carter continued. "She left for Chaseford a week ago today. She said she wanted to catch up with a couple of old friends. She did mention that she was going to visit the cabin in the bush. Our children used to love that cabin."

Assistant Chief Rutherford was amazed by what he'd just heard. Maintaining his composure, he said: "How old is Louise?"

"She'll be 55 on her birthday," said Mrs. Carter. "On July 18th. I do worry about her when she goes away on her trips. She's a single woman. But she usually contacts me by phone to tell me the latest. I don't know what happened this time." Mrs. Carter looked troubled. "She's always been good to me, but I don't see much of the boys. Proctor and Amos are pretty wrapped up in their businesses."

"Do they ever go back to Chaseford to visit?" he asked.

"Good heavens, no," exclaimed Mrs. Carter. "They've made it clear they have no interest in that town. They've been relatively successful and can't imagine why Louise still has any connection to it."

After these revelations, Assistant Chief Rutherford wasn't sure how to proceed. He had some difficult questions for Mrs. Carter.

Sitting quietly across from him for a moment, Mrs. Carter finally looked up and said: "Why are you here, Assistant Chief Rutherford?"

It was an opening which he pursued carefully.

"I was contacted by the chief of police of Chaseford yesterday," he said. "He called me because he's investigating a crime that happened in the bush on the land that you own near Goshawk."

Mrs. Carter looked away. "What kind of crime?" she said.

"A body was found in a cabin."

Mrs. Carter started to weep.

"The chief, Bob Petrovic, hasn't been able to identify the body yet. It's an isolated place. It was only yesterday that the chief was able to determine that the bush belonged to your family. He asked me to contact you."

Mrs. Carter dried her eyes. Though she was extremely pale her voice was steady. "Was it a woman?" she said.

"Yes, a woman in her 50s," Rutherford said gently.

Once again Mrs. Carter broke down. After a minute or two, when she'd somewhat recovered, Rutherford continued.

"We need to identify the body," he said. "Until that time, we can't perform an autopsy. We need the permission of the next of kin. Would you, or a member of your family, be able to come to Chaseford on Monday?"

"At this time, I'm not sure I'm well enough to travel," Mrs. Carter said bleakly. "And Louise's brothers aren't always easy to contact. They don't always get along with me and Louise. I do have a suggestion for you, though: when Louise left for Chaseford she told me she was going to meet up with some of her childhood friends. Her best friend is Alice Chalmers. They've visited back and forth since they were teenagers. Louise told me she was going out to dinner with Alice on Saturday. Alice knows Louise very well. Does Alice serve as a person able to identify her body?"

"I think, under the circumstances," said Assistant Chief Rutherford, "Alice would be a suitable choice. I'll contact Chief Petrovic later today and pass on Alice's name." He hesitated. "I'm very sorry to have brought you this news, Ruth. We won't know for certain whether or not your daughter is the victim until the body has been identified. You'll be contacted immediately after the identification, whether or not it is Louise. If it is Louise, I'd like to be able to tell Chief Petrovic that you've agreed to an autopsy."

Mrs. Carter rang a small bell and Nurse Bella came into the room.

"I most certainly will approve," said Mrs. Carter, now very pale, with Nurse Bella, at her side. "I know this hasn't been easy for you, either, Mr. Rutherford. I appreciate the visit, and the care you took in the way you notified me of the situation. Now, if you don't mind, I think I will retire for a while. Bella, please show Assistant Chief Rutherford out. Then you can help me to my room."

Rutherford thanked Mrs. Carter once more for her graciousness in meeting him on a Saturday then followed Bella to the door.

On Friday, Chief Petrovic had told Rutherford that he needed the latest information for his meeting first thing Monday morning, so that they could plan the next step of the investigation, so he had given Rutherford his home number and requested to be informed as soon as possible after the interview. So as soon as Assistant Chief Rutherford returned to his office, he placed a call to Chief Petrovic's home in Chaseford. Chief Petrovic was very surprised by what he had to say.

Sunday, May 27 and Monday, May 28

CHIEF PETROVIC HAD been restless all day Sunday.

On Sundays, he usually slept in until 8 o'clock, but this Sunday morning he was up by six. The family always went to church together; Sunday school started at 10:00 AM and ran until about 10:45; the church service started at 11:00. His wife taught Sunday school, so she liked to be at the church by 9:30. The Petrovics' church was well attended. The minister was an excellent speaker and most people looked forward to hearing his Sunday sermon. The Petrovics knew this wasn't the case in all the local churches. They had friends of a different denomination that had hinted that the sermon was the one part of their service they could always count on to help them catch up on their sleep.

Bob Petrovic liked to spend Sunday afternoons with his children whenever possible. Their favourite activity was fishing in a local creek. Evidently, however, Mother Nature had decided that this Sunday would be a good time to catch up with her rain quota. The early spring had been drier than usual and the rain was welcome, but it was steady enough that it put a crimp in the Petrovic family's plans. This Sunday, their entertainment would be a 500 piece jigsaw puzzle.

It was a beautiful piece of scenery, Bob thought to himself as studied the box. It showed a farmhouse on the edge of a bush. In Bob's opinion, it looked a lot like Herbert and Emeline Derrigan's place.

Bob knew that this thought had crept into his mind because he couldn't stop thinking about the suspicious death at the cabin. He tried to push it out of his thoughts, at least temporarily, and as they sorted and matched up the pieces, the jigsaw puzzle did help to calm him a bit. But this hard-won tranquility was fleeting. Already, this peaceful family activity was being interrupted by a squabble between his two daughters over who would do the edge pieces. Mother stepped in and decreed that each daughter would get to do one half of the edge pieces. There was to be no hoarding or hiding of edge pieces by anyone, including Dad. Order was restored, and a period of peace ensued.

Bob had calmed down even more by suppertime. But to anyone who knew him, especially his family, it was obvious that something was on his mind. After supper, he and his wife went to the front room, or parlour, as she liked to call it, and turned on their new radio. They had purchased the radio earlier that year. As far as Bob's wife was concerned it wasn't easy to listen to. "Too much static," she said. But it was new and kind of exciting and Bob was proud to own it. Not many people in Chaseford had radios, but you could now buy them locally and they seemed to be the up-and-coming thing. NBC had been set up in the USA two years before and that evening the four of them gathered around to listen to a broadcast from a Detroit station. They heard the A&P Gypsies and then the Voice of Firestone. Then the girls were sent off to bed.

When the two of them were alone, his wife said: "What are you worried about, Bob?"

"I know tomorrow's going to be a very busy day," Bob replied with a sigh. "I just want to make certain I have everything organized in my mind before the start of the day."

"It's about that body that was found at that cabin in the bush, isn't it?" she said.

Bob didn't want to upset his wife with this business, especially since it could involve murder. "I don't want to discuss it," he said. "I can't discuss it with you, even if I wanted to. Let's talk about something else."

Bob's wife had had many conversations of this nature with him before and she knew that when he was wound up like this there wasn't much she could do. It was time to talk about something else. So they did.

After 15 minutes or so Bob said: "My dearest, I'm going to the den to jot down a few notes for tomorrow."

As the chief of police, he did need to be organized. He had a 9 o'clock meeting in the morning with Det. Gerald O'Neill from London. He also wanted to talk to the coroner, Dr. Frank Whittles, and he needed to contact Alice Chalmers to ask her to identify the body. There were some other ongoing police matters as well that he had to fit into his Monday. He was also anticipating a visit from the mayor sometime tomorrow for an update.

Even with the next day organized on paper, Bob still couldn't seem to calm down. The last two days, with the revelations that had come to light, had been too exciting.

He and his wife went to bed at their usual time but he spent the night tossing and turning. He finally got up around 3 in the morning and went downstairs and sat in his favourite easy chair. There was no point in him continuing to disturb his wife's sleep.

MONDAY MORNING HAD arrived. Chief Petrovic knew he had about a week's worth of work to get through by the end of the day.

He got out of his comfortable chair about 6:00 AM, having managed to get a couple of hours' sleep sitting up. This early in the morning, even on a school day, he knew he would have the bathroom to himself for a while. He had a shower and shaved and put on clean clothes for the start of the week. Then he went up to the bedroom and said good morning and goodbye to his wife. Chief Petrovic left the house a little earlier than usual and was down at Mabel's Diner just before 7:00 AM.

The chief had a big breakfast. Bacon and eggs and a couple pancakes with maple syrup. He washed it down with two cups of strong coffee. Mabel was used to seeing the sheriff early Monday mornings. For the last few years, he had made it his habit to have his Monday morning breakfast at Mabel's Diner. The diner wasn't too busy yet this morning, and this gave her the opportunity to ask if there was any new information about that body that had been found in the woods. The chief gave his standard reply: he said that he had no comment to make at this time; he told her it was far too early in the investigation to say anything; he mentioned there were still too many loose ends and too many things to figure out; and he said these things in a voice that was loud enough for several of Mabel's nearby customers to hear. It was a little bit like a radio broadcast and he knew that everyone within earshot was tuned in to hear. Hopefully, everybody would now go back to having their breakfast.

Dr. Frank Whittles appeared and sat down next to the chief at the breakfast counter.

"Good morning, Bob," said the doctor. "Is there anything we need to meet about today? If so, give me a time."

Dr. Whittles knew from experience that any questions he asked of the chief of police in Mabel's Diner had to be carefully crafted. No news would be broadcast without the chief's permission.

"After you're done your breakfast, drop into my office, Frank," said the chief. "We will have a chat then."

For the next few minutes, the breakfast crew spent their time talking about American League Baseball. Almost everyone in the area was either a Cleveland Indians fan or a Detroit Tigers fan. This wasn't a particularly good year for either team. Most of the crew talked about how much they disliked those New York Yankees. The general consensus was that, hopefully, with Cleveland and Detroit out of it this early, the Philadelphia Athletics would win the pennant. Heck, even the St.

Louis Browns were better than the Tigers and Indians this year. With the mention of the St. Louis Browns, the chief got up.

"I've had enough," he declared and went to the till. "Do you have any pies for sale?" he asked Mabel as he was paying his bill. "I know it's Monday. Maybe it's too early in the week?"

"It's never too early for pie, chief," Mabel replied. "I baked some apple pies yesterday."

"That's great!" said the chief. "I'll send Cst. Herman over in half an hour or so to pick up two apple pies."

The chief then headed out the door with Dr. Whittles the coroner close behind.

WHEN THEY REACHED HIS office, he informed his secretary, Sherry Simpson, that he was not to be disturbed while he met with Dr. Whittles. He also told her to put the teakettle on. They would be having some tea at about 10 o'clock.

Chief Petrovic closed the door and turned to Dr. Whittles.

"I want you to keep what I'm about to tell you confidential," he said. "Outside of myself, nobody locally yet has this information."

"Understood," said Dr. Whittles.

"Over the weekend, as a result of some good leg work done by Cst. Herman, we were able to determine the owners of the bush land. They live in the Ottawa area. The officer in charge of criminal investigations in the Ottawa area is Assistant Chief Dick Rutherford. With his help, and as a result of an interview he conducted, we have uncovered some very significant information. I believe the body the boys found in the cabin is the body of Louise Carter."

The coroner was stunned.

"How is that possible?" said Dr. Whittles. "The Carters haven't lived in the area for over 20 years."

"It's a long story," answered the chief. "I have some other news for you as well. We have permission from Mrs. Carter to conduct an autopsy if the body is her daughter's. So all we need to do now is make certain the body is correctly identified. I'll be arranging a meeting with Alice Chalmers sometime later this morning. Alice has been a lifelong friend of Louise Carter, and according to Louise's mother, Ruth, Louise had supper with Alice in Chaseford the day before she died. I'll arrange for her to meet you at the hospital at 1:30 this afternoon so that she can take a look at the body. Will that time work for you, Frank?"

"I'll make it work," said the coroner.

"I don't want to rush you, Frank, but I've got another meeting in a few minutes. At 9 o'clock."

With the prospect of finally being able to conduct an autopsy ahead of him, Dr. Whittles left the office walking purposefully.

Dr. Whittles had been gone for only five minutes when there was a knock on the door. It was still well before 9 o'clock. The chief opened the door and found Det. O'Neill on the other side.

"Hello, Chief. I got up early," said the detective. "I often find a drive in the morning helps me clarify my thoughts. On my way down the highway from London I did some more thinking about how we could conduct our interviews."

"Sounds like you're working overtime," said the chief. "But before we discuss that, I'll alert you that, before the start of our meeting, I want to bring everyone up-to-date on some pertinent developments that occurred this past weekend. But I'd prefer to wait until I have the other constables here before I talk about these developments. Then I won't have to go over things again."

"Not a problem," said Det. O'Neill. "I have some notes here about my interview methods and a list of potential questions. I would appreciate it if you would take a look through this information prior to the meeting."

The chief sat down and read through the material.

"It seems like you're very thorough, Gerald. You obviously have a lot of experience. We certainly appreciate your help."

Just as the chief was finishing his preview of Det. O'Neill's questions there was another rap on the door. It was Cst. Herman.

"Det. O'Neill, I'm pleased to introduce you to one of our constables, Peter Herman," said Chief Petrovic. "I don't think you've met him before. He's the fellow that did the leg work that uncovered the ownership of the bush."

Det. O'Neill raised his eyebrows and smiled. "That must be one of the developments over the weekend you hinted at," said the detective.

The chief winked at Det. O'Neill. "You truly are a detective." He turned to Cst. Herman. "I have an important mission for you," he said. "I'm entrusting you to pick up two apple pies from Mabel's Diner and to deliver said pies safely here, forthwith."

Everyone chuckled as Cst. Herman headed out the door.

"I think I can hear him whistling," said Det. O'Neill.

"He probably is," said the chief. "He loves apple pie, and he really appreciated the compliment I gave him."

Ten minutes later, Cst. Herman was back and Cst. Smith had arrived. It was time for the meeting.

Chief Petrovic started by saying: "Det. O'Neill has worked very hard over the weekend to prepare a list of questions for us to use when we conduct our interviews. He'll explain his strategy when the meeting is turned over to him. But before that, I'd like to start the meeting by bringing everyone up to date on the latest developments over the weekend."

Chief Petrovic then proceeded to outline everything from Cst. Herman's discovery of the ownership of the bush to Assistant Chief Rutherford's visit to Mrs. Carter's home in Ottawa and to the revelations that came from that meeting. The chief told them about his meeting with Dr. Whittles earlier in the morning and explained that if Alice Chalmers could give them a positive identification that would achieve two goals: the victim would be identified, which would be a huge step forward in the investigation; and the autopsy could proceed and hopefully reveal the cause of death.

Det. O'Neill and the deputies were properly impressed.

"Let me congratulate you on your detective work to date, chief," said Det. O'Neill. "With your permission, I will now proceed with my part of the meeting."

The chief nodded.

"I have two items on my agenda," said Det. O'Neill. "To begin with, I would like everyone to take a look at this set of interview questions I've prepared. The order of the questions is important. There *is* a strategy involved. However, during the course of an interview, an answer to one of our questions may prompt you to add a further question we had not contemplated. If you are confident, and it makes total sense to ask your new question, ask it. You may gain significant information. If you have any doubts about asking the question at that time, then make a brief note to yourself and continue with the interview, saving that question for later. We can always go back and interview someone again. If you save the question, then after the interview has been completed, you can come and talk to myself or to the chief and we can give it some consideration. Maybe we can even think of some other questions go with it for a follow-up interview."

A good discussion ensued. Other questions were considered and two were added to the list. They realized Det. O'Neill knew what he was talking about. Because of the new developments in the case, everyone was enthusiastic.

"Before we get to the second part of Det. O'Neill's agenda," the chief interrupted. "I think we need a break for pie and tea."

This was a very popular suggestion. After their brief, 10-minute break, they proceeded with Det. O'Neill's second item.

"I had prepared a list of candidates for interview," said the detective. "But as a result of the events of this past weekend, we will be adding to the list."

So they fleshed out the interview list, which included Jay and Joel, their parents, and farmers that owned properties that abutted the bush. They added all the members of the Carter family and nurse Bella Frankel.

"As we conduct these interviews," said Det. O'Neill, "we may find that other names come up. If so, we will add them to the list. Everyone will do some interviewing. There will always be at least two of us present for every interview."

"You two," Chief Petrovic added, pointing at Csts. Herman and Smith, "will be in charge of contacting the people to be interviewed over the next two days. Some have telephones and some do not. If they do not have a phone, you will have to pay them a visit. You will report the names of those contacted and the interview times back to our secretary, Sherry Simpson. Remember to allow for a reasonable time between interviews. The other excellent recommendation from Det. O'Neill is that the local paper be contacted as soon as possible. We want to know what vehicles or people anyone may have seen in the area of Goshawk on the weekend of the death that were not ordinarily seen in that area. Cst. Herman, please visit the newspaper office once this morning's meeting concludes."

With that, the meeting ended.

ALICE CHALMERS, A STOCKY, friendly woman with a ready smile, was a long-time resident of Chaseford. Her oldest children were gone from home and now had families of their own. The youngest boy, Chad, had just finished his first year at the University of Western Ontario and had a summer job with the newspaper. Alice worked part-time for the newspaper as well. Alice worked afternoons, four days a week, so her meeting with Chief Petrovic, set for 11:00 AM at the police station, was not a big inconvenience. But she had fretted over it a bit. Why on earth, she wondered, would the police want to see *her*? She was sure neither Chad nor her husband were in trouble, but she supposed she would find out the reason for her visit soon enough.

The chief of police at last appeared and escorted her to his office. He offered her a chair and she sat down.

"I'm a little worried – and really curious – why you want to see me," she said.

The chief seated himself with a sigh.

"You're not in any trouble, Alice. Nor is anyone in your family. I know you're all good members of the community. But I do have what will likely be very upsetting news for you." The chief paused, choosing his words carefully. "I think you know that a body was found at a cabin in the bush near Goshawk last weekend. I'm sorry to tell you that we believe the body may be that of your friend Louise Carter."

Alice's demeanour changed abruptly and the colour drained from her face. She was in a state of shock.

"It can't be," she said. "I had supper with her Saturday. Just the two of us."

Chief Petrovic remained silent, giving her a chance to process this unexpected possibility.

"Whenever Louise came to Chaseford," Alice resumed, voice quavering, "we always had a good visit. We had agreed several years ago, you see, that every year, on the Saturday of the Victoria Day holiday weekend, we would go out to supper. Just the two of us." She took a deep, shuddering breath. "That left my husband at home as the cook. For the children. He didn't seem to mind."

Alice broke into a sob.

"I'm very sorry, Alice," said the chief. "I know this is a great shock to you. But we need your help."

Amidst her tears, Alice asked: "H-how can I h-help?"

"One of my colleagues in Ottawa has already spoken to Louise's mother," said Chief Petrovic. "But she's housebound. We need someone to identify the body and she recommended you. Do you think you could do that?"

Alice struggled to answer. "Yes," she said, finally. "I think I can do that."

"Thank you," said the chief. "We appreciate your assistance. Would you be able to meet the coroner, Dr. Whittles, at the hospital at 1:30?"

"I think so," said Alice, recovering somewhat. "I'm supposed to work this afternoon, but they have also been wonderful to me at the newspaper. I think, under the circumstances, it won't be a problem."

"If it is a problem, let me know," said Chief Petrovic. "I'll make the arrangements."

The interview concluded, Alice made a tearful goodbye and left the office.

CHIEF PETROVIC FELT like he had done two weeks' worth of work that morning. Dealing with a murder wasn't an easy thing. Despite his many years of police experience, conversations like the one he'd had with Alice Chalmers were always difficult.

He looked at the clock. It was almost noon. Only half the day was over and already he felt exhausted. He lived only about three blocks from his office and decided he needed a nice, quiet break.

I'll go home and have lunch with my wife, he thought. She'd gone to visit her mother this morning. Asking her how her visit had gone would take his mind off the case.

So Bob went home. He had a bowl of soup and a chicken sandwich. The chicken was left over from Sunday's supper. He and his wife had a pleasant conversation about his mother-in-law. Bob didn't mind his mother-in-law. Her husband had died about two years ago but she seemed to be getting along fine living in her own home. It was the same house that his wife had grown up in.

Chief Petrovic returned to his office just before 1 o'clock. Sure enough, the mayor appeared about 10 minutes later.

Mayor Thompson was a breath of fresh air. He'd won election a year before, and he was a good man. He respected the law and he was easy to work with. More importantly, Mayor Thompson was reliable and he knew how to keep confidential matters confidential. The last mayor had been a bombastic showboat who'd always had to be front and centre. He'd tried to run everything and everybody – even if he didn't know what he was doing. After four years of those antics, he never stood a chance of being reelected. The chief of police didn't like to think about the old mayor. The interfering busybody had almost cost him his job.

Chief Petrovic updated the new mayor on the current status of the case. Mayor Thompson thanked him and reassured the chief that he wouldn't discuss it with anyone else. Then he asked how Det. O'Neill was working out and wondered if there was any other support he could provide to help the chief of police with his investigation. The chief assured him that he would let him know.

The mayor departed and Chief Petrovic turned his attention to some other police matters. He was just finishing up some paperwork when there was a knock on the door. He looked up. It was a little after three in the afternoon.

He went to the door and opened it. Dr. Whittles was waiting on the other side.

"Did you meet with Alice Chalmers?" asked the chief.

"Yes. I've never really spoken to Mrs. Chalmers before," said the coroner. "She's a very nice woman, but now she's also a very upset woman, Chief. She gave us a positive identification on the body. It is Louise Carter."

Chief Petrovic sighed. "Thanks, Frank. I guess now you can do the autopsy, at least."

"Yes. As a matter of fact, I think I'll do some preliminary work right now," said the coroner. "I'll take a brief break for supper and complete the autopsy this evening, if possible. I'm concerned about how much information we'll still be able to obtain from the body. It's been a few days and the body, though still usable, is not in the greatest of conditions."

"Well, let me know as soon as possible how you get on this evening," said the chief. "Call me at home."

Dr. Whittles promised he would and left Chief Petrovic to continue with his own work.

LATE THAT NIGHT, DR. Whittles phoned the chief of police at his home.

"I've examined the body and the internal organs," the coroner said, "and with the limited resources available to me, I can rule out the head trauma as the cause of death. I'm also fairly certain that Louise Carter didn't die from natural causes. I don't know what she did die from yet. With your permission, Bob, I'd like to see if I can get some help with the autopsy. I've heard that there are a couple of doctors practising forensic medicine in Toronto. Forensics is not widely used, yet, but they're occasionally called upon by the Toronto police for difficult investigations. Maybe one of them could help us. Would you be able to phone the Toronto police tomorrow morning to get the name of one of these forensic specialists? Then I can give him a call and talk to him about the autopsy."

"I think that's a good plan, Frank. I'll phone Toronto tomorrow morning and get back to you with a name and number."

"Thanks, Bob."

Dr. Whittles hung up and Chief Petrovic returned to the still incomplete puzzle. It appeared to be missing a piece.

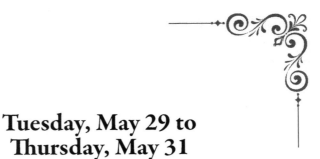

Tuesday, May 29 to
Thursday, May 31

BY 9 O'CLOCK TUESDAY morning, the chief of police had already talked to Toronto, gotten the name and number of a doctor of forensic medicine, and passed it on to Dr. Whittles. Frank was delighted. The doctor's name was Omar Whitehead.

Dr. Whittles contacted Dr. Whitehead immediately. The forensic specialist asked for details regarding the case and then told Dr. Whittles he would be pleased to come to Chaseford to examine the autopsy results. He also mentioned that he may need to take some of the victim's blood, and perhaps part of the body, back to his own laboratory in Toronto for further analysis.

During their conversation, Dr. Whitehead asked the coroner if he had checked for poisoning. Dr. Whittles admitted that he had not and confessed that he didn't have any expertise in that area. He apologized once more for intruding on Dr. Whitehead's schedule.

"Don't apologize," said Dr. Whitehead. "I'm very pleased you were professional enough to understand the limitations of your knowledge. Not everyone is. I'm very happy you called me in for a consult. I'll help you as much as I can. I'll leave Toronto today after lunch and meet you at your local hospital at 3 o'clock. If things go well, we'll have a much better idea of the cause of death by the end of the day Thursday."

Dr. Whittles was pleased that help was on the way.

SHORTLY AFTER 11:00 AM, the chief, the detective, and the two constables sat down at the table in the chief's office. Interviewing was to begin that afternoon. There were to be two teams: Chief Petrovic, assisted by Cst. Smith; and Det. O'Neill, assisted by Cst. Herman.

The chief and Cst. Smith were going to interview the boys, Joel Franklin and Jay Jarvis, as soon as they arrived at the police station after school. They had arranged to meet with Joel's parents later at their home on Durham Street at 7 o'clock.

While they were conducting their interviews, Det. O'Neill and Cst. Herman would be conducting their own interviews. It was a rainy day and, as a result, since it was too wet to work the land, Det. O'Neill and Cst. Herman had been able to set up interviews with Herbert and Emeline Derrigan at their farm starting at 2:00 PM. Det. O'Neill and Cst. Herman would interview Jay Smith's parents later at their home that evening.

Though they all needed to keep an open mind before the beginning of each interview, the four policemen wanted to review all the relevant facts of the case together. It was important that they all start with the same basic understanding of the situation. It was also important that they have no preconceived theories. They didn't yet have enough evidence or information to form a testable theory.

By the time the meeting ended, just before noon, they were ready to proceed with the interviews.

"Before you go," the chief reminded them, "don't forget that all the local interviews are to be completed by Wednesday evening."

WEDNESDAY MORNING, the four investigators met again for a roundtable session to go over the results of their interviews. Had anything new turned up? Had any of the information coming out of the interviews created a need for an adjustment to their questions? If they were going to have a common base from which to consider answers from interview questions, this roundtable session after each day of interviews was crucial.

The interviews of the boys and their parents did not produce anything new, but the interview with Emeline Derrigan did provide a new piece of information that might be relevant.

"It turns out," said Det. O'Neill, "that Emeline Derrigan is Louise Carter's cousin, so she may be able to provide us with information about the Carter family dynamics. Cst. Herman and I did not pursue that connection in our interview, though, because I think we need to conduct our interviews with the Carter family first."

"That sounds very wise," said Chief Petrovic.

"It could be valuable information," said Det. O'Neill. "We don't really know. An older detective that I learned a great deal from used to say: 'sometimes a ripple here causes a wave somewhere else.'"

The chief cleared his throat. "I have some new information for you to consider," he said, turning to the constables. "Det. O'Neill brought a fingerprint report with him from London today. It concerns the two tin cups and whisky bottle that he and Cst. Smith found on the trail near the cabin. We sent them to London to be dusted because they have better facilities there. They found two different sets of fingerprints. One set has already been identified and belongs to Louise Carter. This is a valuable piece of information we don't want anyone else to know about."

The chief paused to let this information sink in.

"Okay," he concluded. "I think we're finished with this meeting. It's been productive. Let's hope today's interviews also produce something significant. Remember, if you don't ask you won't find out. Further, stay alert: keep in mind that what people don't say may be as important as what they do say.

"Unfortunately, we won't be able to have our roundtable session tomorrow morning. Det. O'Neill and I are taking the train to Ottawa and it's going to take us all day to get there. It's going to cost us some time, but it's very important we interview Louise Carter's relatives ourselves; that way, we'll get to meet them and get a first-hand impression of them. And the information will come directly to us instead of being delivered to us by a third party.

"That's it. Meeting adjourned."

With the meeting complete, they were ready to proceed with the day's interviews. They would be on the same teams today. Each team would be interviewing three families. The families lived on farms in close proximity to the bush. The first interviews were slated for two in the afternoon.

THE CORONER, DR. WHITTLES, and the forensic specialist, Dr. Whitehead from Toronto, had been working since late Tuesday afternoon.

They had re-examined the organs that Dr. Whittles had removed from the body and had also done extensive tests on the blood. It was now Thursday afternoon and Dr. Whitehead told Dr. Whittles that they had completed as many tests as they could with the local resources.

At this time, they had ruled out death by natural causes but they had been unable to pin down just why Louise Carter had died. Dr. Whitehead said, based on certain things he'd noticed about some of the brain tissue and blood, that he thought poisoning was involved. They had tested locally for common poisons but hadn't gotten anywhere. Dr. Whitehead said that, with Dr. Whittles's permission, he would take some blood and part of the brain back to Toronto with him for further tests. He had more resources there and would be able to broaden the range of toxins he could test for. Dr. Whittles agreed and thanked Dr. Whitehead very much for his time. He said he looked forward to hearing about any progress he made about determining what type of poison caused the death of the victim.

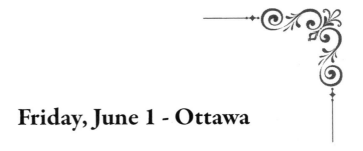

Friday, June 1 - Ottawa

IT WAS JUST AFTER 8 o'clock on Friday morning. Chief Petrovic and Det. O'Neill were sitting down to breakfast at a diner just around the corner from the less than fancy hotel they had stayed at. They were on a limited budget and couldn't afford the best of anything; they were having a tough time affording the second best. But they were pleased with their breakfast all the same. It wasn't quite up to Mabel's standards, but it was good.

"I didn't enjoy that train ride," said the chief over his breakfast. "I've never been on a train ride that long before. I've ridden horses – it's not my favourite pastime, but I can do it – but I've never been on a horse that was as uncomfortable as that train."

Det. O'Neill grinned. "I have to agree with you, Chief. Between the bumping and the rattling, and all the local stops and starts, and more bumping and rattling, it was not a pleasant journey. And just think: tomorrow we get to do it all over again."

"Well, we did get here in one piece, I suppose," said the chief, "and despite the late supper we did get a couple of hours to prepare for today's interviews. I think we have some good questions, but I have a feeling we'll have a lot more questions by the time we finish the interviews. Based on my conversation with Assistant Chief Rutherford last night, our interviews may not be easy.

"You may recall that I phoned Assistant Chief Rutherford on Tuesday, just before we started our local interviews. I'd asked him if he could make arrangements for all the Carters to meet with us at Ruth Carter's home, at about 10 o'clock in the morning. I thought it might be more pleasant and spacious than an interrogation room, and I wanted everyone to feel comfortable while they waited for us to conduct our interviews with each family member. I told him that, at this point in the investigation, we only have four people to interview in Ottawa: Ruth Carter; Amos and Proctor Carter, her sons; and Ruth's nurse, Bella."

"The nurse?" said Det. O'Neill, raising an eyebrow.

"I'm hoping she's nosy," said Chief Petrovic. "Many nurses who serve as companions are. It's important for them to be that way if they're going to be effective at helping their employer. According to Rutherford, Nurse Bella seemed to be a very competent and trusted employee of Ruth's. Her nosiness, or – putting it another way – her *interest* in serving Mrs. Carter, may mean she's privy to a lot of inside family information. Don't forget, she helped Louise Carter run the house."

"Nosy is probably a better description," said Det. O'Neill.

They both chuckled.

"When we arrived last night," Chief Petrovic continued, "I contacted Assistant Chief Rutherford to let him know we were in town and where we were staying. Rutherford informed me that our original interview plan wasn't going to work out. It turns out that Mrs. Carter's sons won't set foot in her house."

Det. O'Neill raised both his eyebrows.

"He spoke to Mrs. Carter first," said the chief, "and she told him both of her sons were welcome to attend her home for the interviews but that she doubted they would agree to come. When Rutherford asked her why, she explained that they'd had a falling out over money after the death of her husband. It seems that Amos and Proctor wanted more than their share of the estate money because they both ran businesses. They didn't think their mother and their sister Louise needed as much money because they had the house and other country property."

"I see," said Det. O'Neill.

"That money rightfully belonged to Mrs. Carter and Louise, of course," the chief continued. "She knew her sons were doing well enough without it. Rutherford tells me she told him that she was polite with her sons, but firm. She also told him that her decision was not well received by her sons. They both told her they would never set foot in her house again and stormed out.

"Mrs. Carter still doesn't understand why they wanted the money so badly, apparently. It was quite a mystery to her. She told Rutherford that since that time, now several years ago, they have had absolutely nothing to do with her or their sister. She hasn't received so much as a birthday card, let alone a Mother's Day gift or a Christmas present. According to Rutherford, she really seemed to be confounded about the whole thing. But since her sons refused to talk with her or Louise, they couldn't solve the problem.

"And it turns out she was right. Rutherford contacted Amos and Proctor and they both refused to attend an interview in their mother's home. They didn't want to be anywhere near her. When he asked them why, they told him it was a private family matter and – rather less than more politely – that it was none of his business. Although, to tell the truth, Rutherford told me, he doesn't think they knew how to be polite. They certainly don't have the interpersonal skills that their father had. So he had to arrange separate interviews with them.

"The way it's set up now," the chief concluded, "we will be interviewing Ruth and Bella in the morning at Mrs. Carter's home, starting at 9:30. Later in the day, at 2 o'clock, we will conduct interviews with Amos and Proctor at Amos's place of business. He has an office in downtown Ottawa that he runs a geological survey company out of. The information I have about Amos Carter from Assistant Chief Rutherford indicates that he's quite well-to-do. His company surveyors have been instrumental in locating some valuable natural resources, it seems. He and his brother Proctor appear to be on good terms with one another and Proctor assured Rutherford that he would attend his brother's office for the interview."

Chief Petrovic and Detective O'Neill finished their coffee.

"It seems," said Det. O'Neill with a grunt, "these interviews may be a little more difficult to conduct than we'd thought. But also more interesting, and perhaps more informative, than the interviews we conducted earlier in the week. Who knows what we'll uncover? I'm glad we have this information from Assistant Chief Rutherford, though. It gives us a bit of insight into the Carter family dynamics."

"Yes, and I think we may dig up a bit of additional information if we interview Bella carefully," said the chief. "By the way, Assistant Chief Rutherford has graciously offered us a car and a driver while we're here in Ottawa. I told him where we were having our breakfast and he said: 'no comment.'" The chief relayed this anecdote with a chuckle. "But he did assure me he would have a local constable by the name of George Brown pick us up here at nine. He said it would take us about 15 minutes to drive to Ruth Carter's from here."

"It's nice to have a chauffeur," said Det. O'Neill, stretching. "We deserve special treatment after that train ride."

They paid for their coffee and breakfast and then the two men headed for the door.

IT WAS A LOVELY JUNE morning with a beautiful blue sky and not a single cloud and Chief Petrovic and Det. O'Neill were enjoying their ride. They were in a particularly nice section of Ottawa, with homes that had large yards that ran all the way to the river. There were no small houses on this street.

It had only taken them 15 minutes to arrive in the neighbourhood from downtown and during that peaceful interlude they had had a pleasant chat with their chauffeur, Cst. George Brown. They found out that the constable had been with the police force for a little over 15 years and that he was delighted with this recent appointment as an aide to Assistant Chief Rutherford. He found the change from routine police work refreshing; now, he could never be sure what his duties would be until he arrived at Assistant Chief Rutherford's office. He might be part of an investigative team, or he could be taking part in a raid. Today was the first time he'd ever been a chauffeur, though. It was the easiest morning he'd had in a long time. Rutherford had chosen Cst. Brown because of his wide range of experience; if the visiting chief and detective needed anything, Cst. Brown would know who to contact or where to get it.

At length, they pulled into a driveway lined on both sides by a low, well-trimmed cedar hedge and parked in front of a large two and a half story home. They got out of the car and went to the door. Mrs. Carter's house looked to Chief Petrovic to have been built in the 1880s.

A woman of about 50, wearing a nurse's uniform, came to the door. She smiled pleasantly and introduced herself as Nurse Bella.

"I'll take you to the living room," she said, leading them from the foyer. "Mrs. Carter is waiting for you there. She would have met you at the door, but she's in a wheelchair."

"If you don't think Mrs. Carter will mind, I'll wait in the kitchen," said Cst. Brown. "That way, if you need me, I'll be handy."

The chief wondered briefly why the constable had selected the kitchen; then he detected the wonderful aroma of fresh baking.

Nurse Bella gave Cst. Brown a warning glance. "You're welcome to coffee and conversation, constable, but keep your hands off the baking."

Nurse Bella showed Cst. Brown to the kitchen and then returned and continued to lead the chief and the detective down the hall to the living room. Ruth Carter was waiting for them there.

Chief Petrovic and Det. O'Neill passed their condolences on to Mrs. Carter and apologized that circumstances required them to meet with her. Mrs. Carter assured them that she understood.

Before proceeding to the interview, Mrs. Carter asked the chief about Chaseford. She was quite interested to know what was going on there. She'd grown up in the region but of course hadn't been there for many years. She mentioned that she'd always received good reports from Louise when she returned from the area. With the mention of Louise's name, Mrs. Carter teared up a bit but quickly recovered herself. Chief Petrovic told her that her husband Hugh was still remembered very fondly in the area.

With introductions and a brief chat out of the way, they felt a little more comfortable with each other and the interview commenced. The interview revealed relatively little new information; most of it had been passed on by Assistant Chief Rutherford the previous evening. When the interview was over, Chief Petrovic told Mrs. Carter he now wanted to interview Nurse Bella. Mrs. Carter informed him that she'd expected as much from her conversation with Assistant Chief Rutherford the previous evening.

"I expect you would like some privacy for that interview," said Mrs. Carter.

"That would be best," said the chief.

"Then I'll have Bella take me out to the back garden," said Mrs. Carter. "It's my favourite place to sit. Especially on a beautiful day like today. I've got a couple of books I'm keen on reading. Do you read, Mr. Petrovic? Maybe you've read one of them? I think I'll start with *The Bridge of San Luis Rey*, by Thornton Wilder. It's had very good reviews. Louise picked up another strange book for me on her last trip. Something called *Steppenwolf*, written by a Herman Hesse." Once again the old woman teared up and once again quickly recovered. "This lovely morning, in my quiet yard, I'll have a good opportunity to delve into these books. And to get some fresh air. I'll get Bella."

Mrs. Carter rang her bell and a moment later Bella appeared. The nurse escorted Mrs. Carter to the back garden and promptly returned. Chief Petrovic inquired if Bella was ready to begin the interview.

Nurse Bella smiled. She said her only concern was leaving Cst. Brown alone in the kitchen with her fresh baking. "But," she added, "he has been warned."

They all laughed. Bella seemed to be in good spirits. That often boded well for an interview.

"Before we start," she said, "I'd like to let you know about a conversation Ruth Carter and I had earlier this morning, before you arrived. Mrs. Carter told me that I could speak to you about anything that was relevant to your interview questions. She said she could think of nothing that I shouldn't talk about. She wants full disclosure."

The chief and detective looked at one another. That was quite an opening statement. This might turn out to be an interesting conversation.

They proceeded with the interview and once the introductory questions were out of the way they got down to important matters. The most important part of the interview, of course, concerned the relationship of Louise Carter to her family members.

"Tell us about the relationship that Louise had with her mother," said Chief Petrovic.

"They had a strong mother-daughter connection," said Bella. "The connection became even stronger after Louise's father died. Ruth and Louise obviously loved each other. I think Louise would have done anything for her mother. I don't think they had any secrets between them. When Louise went on a trip, Ruth was always happy to see her off, but she was even happier to see her come home."

"What was the nature of the trips that Louise Carter took?" asked Det. O'Neill.

"I think Louise just enjoyed travelling," said Bella. "But she always had a purpose in mind. She was quite interested in Canadian and American history, so her travels usually took her to places on the continent where historic events had occurred. She would visit the historic sites and the local museums, and whenever possible she would bring back memorabilia and postcards commemorating the locale and the historic event."

Chief Petrovic found this insight into Louise's character interesting but wasn't sure how relevant it was to their investigation so he posed another question.

"I understand that Louise visited the Chaseford area two or three times a year," he said. "Do you know what her interest was there?"

"Louise had fond memories of growing up and attending school there," said Bella. "She still had many friends there and she loved the property the family owned in that bush. Ruth was quite enthusiastic about it as well. Before her stroke, Ruth visited the property a couple of times with Louise. Louise had that cabin where you found her body built about 10 years ago. It was a quiet hideaway for her; a retreat she could go to when she wanted some peace and quiet. She'd meet with some of her former friends from the Chaseford area there as well at times. She told me once 'it's my secret place', but it wasn't that much of a secret."

Chief Petrovic was surprised by this part of Bella's answer. He'd been led to believe that the cabin was completely unknown to others. Apparently, it wasn't the mysterious locale he'd assumed it to be. He decided that they would have to question the locals about their knowledge of the cabin in subsequent interviews.

Det. O'Neill had been given what he felt was the best question and he asked it now: "Describe the relationship that Louise had with her brothers."

Bella frowned. "It's a good thing Mrs. Carter encouraged me to speak freely," she said. "I'd say the most distinctive thing about their relationship was their mutual dislike. Amos and Proctor are respectively five and seven years younger than their sister Louise and her seniority bothered them. In some ways, Louise had some of the same skills her father had. She was open, friendly, and found it very easy to talk to other people. She was actually interested in them. Once you got to know

Louise, you just knew that she was a good person. Amos and Proctor
don't have her talent for winning people over. Don't be fooled by them
in the interview, though. They're both very intelligent. They're both
university graduates, both self-made men, and both very proud of it.
I think they feel like their sister was favoured over them by their parents. From what I can see that wasn't true but that doesn't change the
way they feel about it. They're both the kind of people who don't think
well of others, though Amos, the older one, may be a little less that way.
They really don't trust other people. If I wanted to use a fancy term,
I'd call it paranoia. I think they're both just a bit like that. When you
first meet them you'll probably think they're both reasonable and intelligent, and you'd be half right. But don't cross them. I've always been a
little bit afraid of Amos and Proctor. They're big men and they're not
always polite. I've never seen them raise a hand against anybody but
they are intimidating. It's been very obvious since I started working for
Ruth that they don't like either their mother or their sister. And it's
something I just don't understand."

"Was there any specific problem you can think of that might have
caused the disagreement between Louise and her brothers?" asked
Chief Petrovic.

"Well, they considered her travelling and her interest in history a
waste of time and money. It could get expensive, you know. And if *she*
wasn't going to work then she should at least make her *money* work.
Meaning: she should make her money work for them. I know they
wanted her to invest in their companies. And I know she politely told
them she preferred *not* to invest in their companies.

"The other major disagreement I know about was over the bush
land near Chaseford. She loved that land and said that, as long as she
was alive, it wasn't going to be sold. Her brothers saw that land as a
waste. Four thousand acres of land, most of it bush, sitting there doing
nothing. You couldn't grow crops on it and even though it was a big
bush it wasn't worth the money and equipment it would have taken to

harvest the trees. They felt pretty strongly that it should be sold and the money put into their business enterprises. They had a business bee in their bonnet."

By this point, the interview had lasted quite a while, and, although a lot of interesting information had come to light, Chief Petrovic and Det. O'Neill knew it had to be terminated so that they could get on with the rest of the day. They had the brothers' interviews slated for the afternoon. They thanked Bella for her assistance and informed her that they may want to interview her again at some point.

Bella stood up and asked if they would go to the garden to say goodbye to Mrs. Carter.

"We'll take the door from the kitchen to the garden," she said. "There's a door there that leads to the yard. I have to go there anyway to check on my baking. I want to make sure it's safe."

As they entered the kitchen, Cst. Brown stood abruptly, brushing cookie crumbs from his uniform.

"Thank goodness we have the police to protect us from crime," Bella said wryly.

Cst. Brown blushed.

"Mrs. Carter is just through that door," said Bella, pointing.

The lawmen proceeded through the door at the far end of the kitchen into the garden.

Mrs. Carter, sitting in the shade, looked up from her book, smiled, and then set it down in her lap. They thanked her for her cooperation and bid her goodbye. It was about 11:30 AM.

THEY DIDN'T HAVE A lot of time for lunch, but Cst. Brown said he knew a place, not far from the location of their next set of interviews, where they could get excellent homemade soup and sandwiches served with fried potatoes and salad.

"It's not fancy," said the constable, "but it's good and it's economical."

"Sounds like the kind of place my budget likes to go," said Chief Petrovic.

The lunch was as good as the constable had promised and the service was friendly. Chief Petrovic and Det. O'Neill complemented Cst. Brown on his recommendation.

"Say, George, you don't happen to have any extra cookies with you, do you?" asked Det. O'Neill.

Cst. Brown flushed. "Bella said I could have some of her cookies. I just wasn't allowed to touch any of the other baking. And I didn't."

"You're a credit to the uniform, George," said Det. O'Neill.

They all laughed, although Cst. Brown didn't seem quite as enthusiastic as the others.

"If you're done interrogating the constable, detective, we should probably be on our way," said Chief Petrovic.

They left the diner and five minutes later Cst. Brown was pulling the car to a stop in front of a three-story building on one of the main streets of Ottawa. Their timing was almost perfect.

The sign above the door read **Carter's Surveys Inc**. They climbed out of the car and entered through the front door, arriving in a reception area. There they were met by a large man, about six foot four and likely over 250 pounds. He had a neatly trimmed black beard the same colour as his hair.

"Thank you for being prompt," said the man, smiling at them. "I'm Amos. My brother Proctor is here as well, in one of the offices. I assume you'd like to interview us one at a time. Unless you'd prefer otherwise, I'm volunteering to go first. I have some clients I should get ready for that are meeting me here later in the afternoon. If you'll excuse me for a moment, I'll go and let Proctor know that you're here. If it suits your purposes, we can use the first office down the hall on your left for the interviews."

With that, Amos Carter turned and disappeared down the hall. Cst. Brown took a chair in the reception area.

"He's kind of impressive," said Det. O'Neill, turning to Chief Petrovic. "He obviously likes to be in charge. Let's see what kind of an interviewee he is."

The chief of police and the detective walked into the office Amos Carter had suggested. The room had a lot of filing cabinets, a fair-sized table, and four chairs.

"This looks like a good room to use," said Det. O'Neill, looking around.

They were joined less than a minute later by Amos who immediately sat down in one of the empty chairs.

"How can I help you gentlemen of the law?" he said.

Chief Petrovic and Det. O'Neill seated themselves and the interview began.

They always started their interviews with a few easy questions. These questions were used to identify who the people being interviewed were, what they did for a living, and how they were connected to the investigation. With these preliminaries out of the way, they would proceed to some tougher questions. While the primary interviewer asked questions and tried to maintain eye contact with the person being interviewed, the second interviewer acted as a recorder and observer, jotting down answers and watching for any subtle body language or facial expressions expressed by the interviewee.

In Chief Petrovic's opinion, the interview was going well. Amos Carter did not appear to be uncomfortable, he answered their questions succinctly, and when asked he would elaborate.

When asked about his mother and his sister, Amos said: "To others they seem to be very nice people, but my brother and I don't get on with them at all. When our father was alive we were all cordial. He was a great peacemaker. And a man with ideas. He helped Proctor and me a great deal when we were setting up our businesses. When he died, Proctor and I naturally assumed, being the men of the family, that we would be making the decisions and building on his legacy. Our mother, Ruth, and sister, Louise, informed us in no uncertain terms that we were mistaken. They could look after themselves, thank you very much. So we let them."

Det. O'Neill had had a hunch which he'd discussed with Chief Petrovic over lunch and he pursued it now.

"What do you think about your mother's nurse, Bella?" he said.

It was a wide-open question but they were curious to see where Amos went with it. Amos's face coloured a bit.

"I'll say it as nicely as I can," he said. "She's an interfering busybody. She's always offering opinions, even when she's not being asked. I think she's given some very poor advice to both my mother and my sister."

"What's your opinion of the bush?" the chief interjected. "The property with the cabin where your sister's body was found?"

It was a quick change in direction for the interview but Amos had calmed down.

"Simply put?" said Amos. "That bush is of no use to anyone."

"How did your father obtain the bush?" asked Chief Petrovic, curious.

"That bush has been in the Carter family since the early 1800s," said Amos. "But it holds no sentimental value for me. To me, it's just a useless piece of land. The country near Chaseford was where my great-great-grandfather Titus settled. There are still many Carters in the area. One of them lives right next to the bush. Emeline Derrigan. She's my cousin."

The interview continued for another five minutes then the chief ended it and thanked Amos.

"Thank you for interviewing me first," said Amos, rising. "I should still have plenty of time to get ready for my meeting later this afternoon. I'll get Proctor and send him to you."

Amos left and closed the door.

Once Amos was gone, Det. O'Neill turned to the chief.

"He's a pretty cool customer," said the detective. "I can see why he's so successful. Well spoken, but with a bit of a ruthless edge."

"We did get some good information," said the chief.

There was a knock on the door and the man they assumed was Proctor was invited in by the investigators.

Proctor was similar in appearance to Amos but was two years younger, perhaps an inch shorter, and carried a little less weight. He was clean-shaven but had a moustache. Their faces were similar enough that it was easy to recognize that Amos and Proctor were brothers.

In their introductory questions, the chief and detective asked about Proctor's own business. Amos's brother had started out with a small lumberyard and now owned lumberyards in Ottawa, Toronto, and Montréal. As the interview progressed, it became obvious that he was less confident than Amos and seemed to be a nervous person. From his demeanour, one might even say that at times he appeared shifty. He didn't avoid answering any of their questions though. When they got to the relationship with his mother and sister his response was very similar to the answer Amos had given. When asked about Bella, however, he looked down.

"I liked Bella," he said. "We were friends. I've known her for several years. She's a very competent person and a good nurse. When my mother had the stroke, I encouraged Bella to apply for the position of caregiver. I never told my mother or my sister about that, though, so unless Bella said something they were never aware of my recommendation. Once she got the position I gradually got cut off from her. My brother Amos said 'good riddance', though. He doesn't like Bella at all."

"Proctor," said Chief Petrovic, moving the interview along, "you're a lumber man. What do you think of the bush near Chaseford?"

Proctor paused. "It's none of my business," he said finally. "My father left that bush to my mother and Louise. He did that even though he helped me set up my first lumber yard. That bush meant something to him, though, and I guess he didn't want to see it tampered with. Sitting as it is now, it's not of much use."

"Do you know anything about the cabin?" said Det. O'Neill.

"I didn't even know there was a cabin in the bush until I read about it in the paper," said Proctor.

The chief stood up. "Thank you very much for your time, Proctor. If there's any need for a further interview, we'll let you know."

Proctor rose from his chair, smiled nervously, and headed out the door.

Chief Petrovic and Det. O'Neill made their way back down the hall and Amos emerged from his office and they thanked him for his hospitality. When they arrived at the reception area, Cst. Brown got out of his chair and the three of them exited the building.

"George, find us a good place for a coffee," said the chief when they got in the car.

"I know just the spot," said Cst. Brown.

He drove a couple blocks, turned right, went half a block down, and pulled up in front of a small restaurant. They got out and went in. It was a pleasant, brightly decorated place with booths.

"Perfect, George. We can talk here," said Chief Petrovic.

"Do you want me to take a different booth?" asked the constable.

"No, that's okay," said the chief. "Sit with us."

"Before you order your coffee, I feel it's my duty to inform you that they make great doughnuts here," said Cst. Brown.

"I'm glad you're our chauffeur, George," said Det. O'Neill.

Once their coffee had arrived, they had a good discussion. Chief Petrovic and Det. O'Neill were pleased to have uncovered some new information. The Carter brothers had agreed on some things, but they certainly differed in their opinion of Bella.

"Very interesting interviews this afternoon," said the chief. "But there are two things that stand out in my mind: first, that I didn't detect any concern about the fact that their sister may have been murdered;

and second, I didn't detect any concern at all about how their mother must feel. That's unusual, especially considering her dependent condition."

They finished their coffee, purchased some additional doughnuts to take with them, then had Cst. Brown drive them back to the hotel.

When they arrived at the hotel, they thanked the constable for his services and Chief Petrovic told him he would put in a good word about him with Assistant Chief Rutherford. Cst. Brown left and Chief Petrovic and Det. O'Neill arranged to meet again that evening after supper to summarize what they'd learned from the interviews. That would help them decide what would be the next step in the investigation. They had a train to catch early the next morning.

Friday, June 1 - After the Storm

I BECAME AWARE SLOWLY. At first, I wasn't certain where I was. Had I fallen asleep? I couldn't say. I felt unusual, that was for sure.

What happened?

Everything was dark. Quiet. Then I thought I heard a noise.

Who is that?

I must have been waking up. I didn't feel well. It must have been my dad.

Why is my dad waking me up?

Usually, I got myself up. I never had a problem getting up on time. I had an alarm clock, but I usually woke up before the alarm sounded anyway. Things didn't seem right this time.

What's wrong? Why do I feel so strange?

My head was really bothering me. Everything seemed confusing. I was disoriented. I'd heard about strokes. My aunt Addie had had one. She had died a day later.

I'm pretty healthy for 17. I couldn't be having a stroke.

On top of the confusion, I suddenly felt a severe pain in my lower right leg.

My leg was resting against one of the steel legs of the small cot I slept on. I thought I heard my dad's voice, but it seemed a little muted.

This doesn't make any sense. What is my dad doing in the attic?

I couldn't see very well.

Is it morning? It's still dark. Why is he waking me up?

I heard my mom coming up the stairs. She was crying. Something must have happened. But nothing seemed to fit together.

Someone put something cold on my head. I could hear my parents' voices. Someone was trying to sit me up.

Why won't they just let me sleep? I'll feel better when I wake up.

I could see a little better now. The daylight was gone. There was a lantern shining in the attic. I could make out my dad now. I could see him quite clearly. My mom was there too. They were talking to me.

I tried to concentrate. I still wasn't sure what they were saying to me. My head hurt, and the pain in my leg was severe.

"Can you hear us? Nod your head if you can hear us, Joel." It was my dad.

I slowly nodded my head. My eyes were working a little better now and so were my ears.

"Can you talk?" said my dad. "Just answer with a simple yes."

I licked my lips, flexed my cheeks, and got my tongue in the right place.

"Yes, I can hear you," I said.

"What day is it?" said my dad.

I frowned, trying to remember. My mother started to cry.

"It's Friday," said my dad.

"Why is it so dark in here?" I said. "What's wrong with the lights?"

"It's night," he replied. "Do you remember anything about Friday?"

"I don't know," I said. "I know if it's Friday, I probably went to school. And then I probably went to the store. But I don't know. I don't remember. Why is it dark? I'm in the attic. I'm in my room. That's all I know."

"Your thinking seems okay, Joel," said my mom. "You are in your attic bedroom. And it's dark because it's almost 10 o'clock at night."

"So was I at the store?" I said.

"Yes," said my dad. "We know you were there because we stopped to check on the store on the way home and found everything in order.

The store was locked up properly. We were really fortunate there wasn't any damage."

"Damage? Why would there be damage at the store?" I said.

"Chaseford was hit by a very bad storm," said my mom. "Earlier this evening. There's quite a bit of damage. Most of it from the wind. Tree limbs are down and some of the fences have been knocked over. Even some trees have been blown over. The winds were extremely strong. But it wasn't a full tornado, thank heavens."

When my mom was a girl, their farm had been hit by a tornado. They'd lost their barn and their farmhouse and quite a bit of livestock, but no one in the family had been injured because they'd hidden in the storm cellar. Since that time, a tornado was my mother's greatest fear.

"Tonight we lost the big maple at the end of our garden," my mom said, sighing. "The wind didn't get it, but the lightning did. We were lucky it missed the house. And the neighbour's house, too."

"There was an awful lot of lightning," said my dad. "Very severe. Four fires broke out around town. Fortunately, only two of them were in homes. And they were put out by the fire department before they could do any serious damage. Other than that, a small shed and a garage burned to the ground. It's the worst lightning anyone around here can remember. That lightning that took out our maple also caused some minor damage to the house next door. It struck pretty close to our house. I want to have a good look when the sun comes up to see whether our home sustained any damage. Mrs. Jensen from across the street said that it looked like a great big fork of lightning hit our house. Like there was lightning all around it. But it must have been the big maple tree in the side yard that she saw being hit. She was pretty shaken up by the whole thing."

By this point, I was starting to feel a little bit better. But my leg still hurt and my head still felt peculiar. I could see okay now, and my hearing was almost back to normal, but I still felt strange.

"Do I look okay?" I asked my dad. "Take a look in my eyes."

"You look okay, Joel," my dad replied. He gave me a reassuring smile. "You're just a little woozy and not quite yourself."

My mind was clearing and I realized that I was lying on the floor.

"Are you well enough to stand up?" asked my dad.

"I think so," I said. "But my leg hurts a lot."

"Let me look at your leg before you try to get up," said my mom. "Where does it hurt?"

I lifted my pant leg above my calf and pointed.

"See that weird spot? Just above my ankle? It's really painful."

My dad helped me sit up on the edge of the bed. From this position, my mom was able to get a better look at the angry looking spot on my lower leg.

"That looks like a bad burn," she said.

"How could I get a bad burn? There's no sign of a fire."

"Look at the metal support leg of the bed," said my dad. "The paint is peeling off. It wasn't like that before. There's also some minor discolouration. I don't see any other signs of damage, but maybe you got hit by lightning, Joel. If that's the case, I think we're all very lucky. The lightning must have gone from your ankle to that metal support, travelled through the bed frame, and then found another conductor." He pointed along the bed to show me.

"Now that you mention, it sure *hurts* like a burn," I said.

"You need to put something on that burn right now," said my mom. "I've got a remedy for burns that I bought at the drugstore a week ago. Let's try that. If the burn doesn't start to get better in the next few days, then we're going to have to take you to the doctor. But let's try the salve first. It's Friday night and we have the weekend ahead of us. I'm sure you'll be fine for school on Monday."

"Okay," I said, slumping somewhat.

My mom must've recovered from her shock; she was already reminding me about school.

"I'm still kind of foggy about what happened today," I said. "Why are we using the lantern? It looks like you've got one on the second floor, too. Why don't we turn on the lights?"

"Have you heard anything we've said, Joel?" asked my dad. "You look better, but are you taking things in? The wind took down a lot of power lines. It'll probably be two or three days before they have everything up and running in town. Let's go down to the kitchen. We can put the lantern on the kitchen table and have a cup of tea and talk some more."

Mom agreed and we headed down to the kitchen. My brother and sister joined us and we all sat around the table.

"That exercise going down the stairs helped," I said. "I think the fog's lifting. I'm starting to remember what happened. I remember going to school. I felt good because it was Friday. Then I went to the store to look after things, like I usually do. When I got there, you went home to pick up Emmylou and Ralph. The four of you were going to the church picnic.

"Things are coming back pretty clearly now. I left at 7:00 PM, closing time, and went home. On my way home, I could see that there was a storm coming. I decided to relax and sit on the front porch for a few minutes to watch the sky. As the storm got closer, I could hear the thunder and see lightning way off in the distance. The sky got dark enough to be evil and that's when I got really nervous about the storm. I guess you could say I was pretty uneasy. I've been feeling that way now and then since Jay and I found the body in the bush.

"Things didn't seem quite right. I felt kind of scared. And weird. So I came in the house and went up to my room. I got to the attic just about the time the storm arrived. It really was a heck of a storm. I remember the lightning, now, and all the noise. The storm was so loud, blowing against the house, and the lightning was so vicious, tearing up the sky. It bothered me so much that – I'm kind of embarrassed to say – I wanted to hide. Then there was a really bright flash and a noise that was louder than I could bear. And that's the last thing I remember. That must have been when I lost consciousness.

"You know, now that I think about it, I do remember one other strange thing: when that lightning struck, I thought I heard a voice. It seemed to come from somewhere in the attic. I heard it just before I blacked out."

"What did it sound like?" said Ralph, entranced.

"It sounded like a man. He said something like: 'I don't believe it. Who are you? Are you Joel?' Maybe my memory of the storm isn't too good. Did any of you see anybody else in the house when you came home?"

The four of them looked at each other and all shook their heads negatively.

"I think your imagination might be getting the better of you, Joel," said my dad. "You were right to be scared by that storm, though. You could have been hurt a lot worse than you were. And you've had a very difficult week. I'm not surprised you're feeling unsettled. But there's nobody else here and there's no sign of anybody else having been here while we were gone. It was a pretty bad storm. People weren't out wandering around in it."

"Tell him about the picnic," said my mom.

My dad gave her a grim smile. "A little after 5 o'clock, everyone was at the park, just below the pavilion. The tables were all set up, and the Ladies' Auxiliary was busy decorating, setting the tables, and getting the goodies ready. The meal was supposed to start at 6 o'clock, and that left almost an hour for a ballgame and other kids' activities.

"There was a really good turn out. The younger people had lots to do and the older people had lots to watch and plenty of time to chat. The baseball game was the highlight for Ralph."

Ralph grinned at me. He loved to play baseball and he was good at it.

"Emmylou was having a good time running around with the other girls," my dad continued. "When they weren't laughing, they were squealing. Lots of hijinks."

Mom and dad both smiled.

"We got cleaned up and sat down to eat at about five after six," he continued. "After the blessing, we got to enjoy some first-rate food. I think most of us probably ate too much. Just as we were finishing dessert, we heard the first rumbles of thunder. Everyone could see the big, black thunderhead coming straight toward us. The minister said 'I guess the picnic is over. Time to pack up.' He could see we didn't have a lot of time. By the time we got the tables cleared off and the picnic baskets and other hampers packed the rain had started. I should say 'the hail started.'"

"Hail?" said Joel.

My dad held out his hand, with his fingers separated. "The pellets were big. Size of a pea. They came down so fast and furious that we were all yelping and cursing, even though it was a church picnic. We raced to the new pavilion for protection. Remember that controversy last year about spending money on the pavilion in the park? Well, we were all in favour of the spending right then.

"We'd just gotten in when the wind came. Thank God for those strong supporting walls they'd installed as part of the pavilion design. Even with that protection the storm was frightening. You don't need to feel embarrassed about wanting to hide because I can tell you we all wanted to hide right about then.

"As we stood there, huddled in the shelter of the pavilion, we saw a couple of small trees go down. People started praying out loud for our survival, and for the survival of the town. After about half an hour of anxious waiting, the wind finally died down, the lightning became a little more infrequent, and the rain stopped. With a good deal of relief, we said our goodbyes, wished each other a safe journey, and set out for home.

"It wasn't easy. The streets were flooded and the going was slow. By the time we got downtown to the store it was around 8 o'clock. It had taken longer than we anticipated because of the downed trees and the wires laying across the road. There were no lights and it was still so overcast it seemed like night had come early. We had less than a mile to go, but even that was a bit of a challenge. We passed one of the houses that had been set on fire. It's only two blocks from here. We finally arrived home around 9 o'clock, just grateful to see the house still standing and relatively undamaged.

"When we came in the front door, we saw your knapsack in the hallway, so we knew you'd made it home. We called your name a few times but we didn't get an answer. The house was pitch black inside so we set Ralph out to the garage to get the kerosene lanterns. Once we had some light, we started looking for you. Emmylou came running up to your mom and said: 'I think he is in the attic. I peeked over the edge at the top of the stairs, between the railings, and I saw him lying there by the bed. I didn't want to go all the way up because I was scared.'"

Emmylou nodded, looking very solemn.

"That brings you up to date," said my dad. "That was a long story. I think I need to drink my tea."

"How's your head?" said my mom, still looking concerned.

"I feel okay now," I said. "My head still feels different, but I guess I'm talking okay. And I guess I sound okay and I'm making sense. And you're making sense. So, I'm okay. I think that salve is even helping the burn. I feel so good, actually, I think I'm hungry."

"Good, because I'm hungry too," said my dad. "Fortunately for us, your mom kept a cherry pie at home. So let's have a piece of that pie and another cup of tea."

Mom served us each a slice of pie and we chatted about other things. Finally, my dad said:

"Well, I think we should probably hit the sack. And hope for some sweet dreams to shake off this storm."

I hoped my dreams would be sweet but to be honest I was worried. I just couldn't get that other voice out of my head.

Friday, June 1 - First Contact

I LOVED MY ROOM IN the attic. A little over a year ago, I'd been getting a little tired of sharing a bedroom with my brother Ralph, who is five years younger than me. He was always bugging me and getting in the way. So my mom and dad talked it over and thought they could make part of the attic into a bedroom for me. It was a great idea, and after they'd proposed it, I'd looked forward to having my own space and a little privacy. The headroom wasn't the greatest, but in the middle of the attic, where the peak was highest, I could stand at full height. I just had to remember there was a low sloping ceiling everywhere else. The room can get hot in the summer, and cold in the winter, but with the attic door off the temperatures are a little better. We're burning a little more coal and wood in the winter than we used to, to keep me warm, but mom thinks it's a small price to pay for brotherly love.

Tonight, for the first time since I got my own room, I was nervous. I really didn't want to talk to my parents about 'the voice' again. They had already written that off as something my imagination had created in response to the stress of the storm and the finding of the body in the cabin last week. But *I* hadn't written it off. I *had* heard that voice and I knew I would recognize it if I heard it again. I was just hoping that I *wasn't* going to hear it again. I didn't want bats in the attic *or* bats in my belfry. But, you know, you don't always get what you want. Sometimes your mind just won't rest. Especially if there's a mystery involved.

In this case, the mystery was a voice. And my mind was feeling anything but restful.

Nevertheless, I took a flashlight and went up to my room. I looked around the attic, sweeping the flashlight here and there just to make sure I didn't have a guest. Despite finding myself alone, I was still very nervous. I couldn't quite confess to myself that I was afraid, but I was.

I'll read for a little while, just to calm down, I thought. *Maybe I'll get tired enough to fall asleep? I hope that flashlight lasts for a while, though, because I really don't want to turn it off.*

I picked up my favourite book, *The Boy's Own Annual.* It came from England. I'd received a bound copy of the 1927 Boy's Own Papers this past Christmas. When the 52 weekly papers are bound together, they call it the Annual. That's what my dad told me, anyway. The *Annual* was one of my prize possessions, but tonight I thought I would stay away from the adventure stories. Instead, I would read the nature articles and take a look at some of the puzzles. It's a pretty hefty volume, so there was a lot of information to keep my mind occupied.

I started reading an essay on telescopes by a famous British astronomer. He'd kept the language simple and it was interesting and easy to read so I found myself beginning to relax. And then I thought I *felt* something.

I stopped reading and picked up my flashlight and shone it around the attic space. From where I was sitting, I didn't really see anything; but I couldn't get rid of the feeling that something was nearby. The feeling was strong enough that the hairs on the back of my neck and my arms stood up. I knew that was a response to perceived fear – I'd read that somewhere as well, too – but that rational thought wasn't comforting. What did I have to fear in my own bedroom? I was in a secure space. I had my flashlight. We had checked the house carefully before we went to bed and I knew there was no one else here but my family. What could I possibly fear?

But fear, I knew, isn't rational. You don't have to have a reason to be fearful to be afraid. Still, normal, healthy, average people don't go around feeling as though something bad is about to happen. I certainly felt that way at the moment.

Just calm down, I thought to myself.

And that's when I heard my name.

"Joel."

It was the voice. I didn't know what to say. I didn't want to say anything. I didn't want to start talking to people who weren't there. I didn't want to disturb my parents and my brother and sister who were sleeping on the floor below.

"Is your name Joel?" I heard the voice say. It wasn't very loud, but I could plainly hear it. I wasn't imagining things. It was a man's voice.

With great trepidation, I whispered: "Yes."

"I thought so," said the voice.

I didn't know what to do so I said: "Why am I hearing a voice?"

"Because I'm speaking to you," said the voice matter-of-factly.

"Can anybody else hear your voice?" I replied. "Can my parents or the rest of my family hear you?"

"I don't think so," said the voice, sounding thoughtful. "Don't be frightened. I'm as surprised to be talking to you as you are. I really didn't expect to communicate with anyone who was alive again."

This last statement did not make me feel less apprehensive.

"What do you mean by that? Are you a ghost? Don't ghosts try to scare people?"

"I've tried," the voice responded. "Not to scare people, but to communicate. But they can't seem to hear me. You are the first. Please call me Walter. My full name was Walter Yost."

"If I whisper can you hear me?" I said.

"I can hear you if you think about me," said Walter. "You don't have to speak out loud. Just imagine speaking to me in your mind."

"Am I crazy?" I asked him. "Why is this happening?"

"I'm puzzled too," said Walter, "but I think I may know the answer."

"I'd love to hear it, Walter," I said.

"You were struck by lightning," said the voice.

I was dumbfounded by this and didn't know what to say. I was terrified. Was I rational?

"Since my death, I haven't communicated with any other living person," said Walter, "though I have had very limited contact with others like myself."

"So *are* you a ghost?" I said.

"Maybe. I guess it depends on what a ghost is," said Walter, who seemed reluctant about the label. "I know you and your family have never seen me, and I think if you shine your flashlight around now you still won't see me. I think the only reason you and I are communicating at all is that you and I were both in this attic when that tremendous lightning bolt shook everything up. It took out that big tree in the yard and messed up anything relying on electrical signals in the immediate area, including your mind, which runs on electrical impulses. You have that burn on your leg as proof and as a reminder. But I'm sure your mind was affected too. I have no rational explanation as to how we can communicate, though. For all intents and purposes, in your world, I don't exist.

"I didn't die peacefully," Walter continued. "I died in a terrible accident. Before that, I went through a situation that was very unfair and frustrating and it left me in an almost permanent state of anger. Perhaps I was so angry, as I lay dying, that I just refused to just stop existing. I'll briefly tell you my story. It won't explain why we can communicate, but it will show you how we came to be in such close proximity.

"I'll start with my family. I grew up on a small farm not far from Chaseford. I had one older brother. He left home as soon as he could. He moved out of the area and my parents never saw him again. We were very poor and my dad was a heavy drinker. That's likely why my brother left. In 1915, when I was 28 years old, I decided to fight for Canada and proudly joined the Army. I wasn't married and the war needed soldiers. I was sent overseas, and then to the front lines, where I saw a lot of killing. It was the 'war to end all wars'. I don't think it did. There'll probably be another one. Up until that time, I'd worked the farm with my father and mother. My father told me that, if I joined the service, he would quit drinking and that he'd be able to manage the farm. I don't think I believed him but I left anyway. If the next tragedy hadn't occurred, I'd likely have come back to the farm. I'd be out there farming instead of talking to you.

"After I left, my dad drank even more. I know he didn't do much on the farm. I don't how my mom survived. They couldn't even pay the taxes. Then one night in the winter of 1918, when I was overseas, the farmhouse caught fire. Both my parents died in the fire. When my sergeant notified me, I pretty well went berserk. They had to lock me up for a couple of days. I was informed my older brother was looking after things. He arranged a funeral and my parents were buried. Then he sold the farm to pay past taxes. There was nothing left.

"After I got back from the war, I didn't know what to do. I didn't have a family. I never did see my brother again. I didn't even have a place to live. My only solace was my anger. Anger is a jealous friend. When you're angry, you don't have any other friends. The one good thing was that I didn't turn to alcohol. I didn't want to be like my father.

"After I'd been back in the area for about a week, I did get a lucky break. I'd been sleeping in the basement of one of the local churches at night and during the day I was going around town trying to find any work I could. When I came back to the church one Tuesday evening the minister said: 'Bob Jones tells me he could use an extra hand at his sawmill'. The next morning I walked out to the edge of town to Jones Lumberyard.

"Bob Jones hired me on the spot, bless his heart. He also found me a place to stay. That's how I came to live in this house. It was late in 1919 when I moved in. The Spencers owned the house then. They charged me for room and meals and I even got a packed lunch for work. Things were improving. I started to lose the edge off my anger. I became a good employee for Bob Jones. My life had turned around. Then the fateful day January 23, 1922, arrived.

"That's when I had the accident. I was moving some lumber around in the upper storage area. We had just rough cut some trees into 2-inch-thick pieces. I was on the storage platform above the work area. I stumbled and fell from the work area onto one of the big saw blades below. That blade cut my arm off just above the shoulder. I bled to death before they could even get me to the hospital. The Spencers held a wake for me in this house. I was laid on the table right down there in the living room. Maybe all that tragedy was too much for my soul. My soul is not at rest. And I have never left this house.

"I know there are others like me. It's a small number. The only ones I've encountered also suffered a traumatic death. They were murdered or terribly betrayed. Maybe that rage is what prevents those few of us from leaving. There are even a few living people like you around who have been in contact with a ghost. I'll use the word 'ghost' because I don't know what other word to use. I don't know what has given other living persons this ability to be receptive to being contacted by a ghost, but I know not many living people are so unfortunately fortunate. In your case, lightning seems to have triggered a latent ability that makes your mind highly sensitive to its surroundings. The good thing about this sensitivity, according to others with your ability, is that you have control over it. Otherwise, your heightened senses would continually bombard your mind and you would go crazy. If you learn to focus this ability your perception of your surroundings will be far greater than a normal person's. You will have a greater visual acuity, a wider range of hearing, a greater sense of smell and touch. But only when you choose to use it."

"What about you? Are you friendly? Are you evil? Can you hurt me?" I asked.

"I could ask you the same questions," said Walter. "I'm pretty sure we would both would provide the same answers. But ultimately it doesn't matter because I don't really exist in your world so I'm not sure how I could hurt you. You can communicate with me, and I can communicate with you when you wish it; but otherwise your life goes on as before. I guess the main advantage you've gained in having met me is that I've been able to provide you with some understanding of the ability you may now have.

"You may also want to be able to communicate directly or indirectly with others that share your abilities. I really only know one other person like you and she seems pretty normal. At least, she hasn't gone mad, and I would say she lives a fairly ordinary life. But we don't communicate very often. Matter fact, I really don't communicate with her at all. Another 'ghost' is her intermediary. You're the only one that I can communicate with directly and I think that this bizarre occurrence happened because of the pure coincidence of you and I being in close proximity in your room when lightning struck."

This is really weird, I thought. "Walter, can you read my mind?"

"Only when there's a connection established between us. And that will depend on you," he said.

"What happens if I tell other people about you, Walter?"

"Nothing happens to me," said Walter, "but I'm not sure what would happen to you. You don't seem like the kind of person that wants to go into show business or join the circus. You don't seem like the kind of person who would try to turn this into a moneymaking opportunity. Who knows? You have pretty good communication skills, and maybe you would be able to convince other people you really are in contact with me, but they won't hear me and they won't see me so your credibility may be suspect. Your story will not sound very believable to most people. It won't sound normal.

"Most likely, one of two things may happen: people may just laugh at you, or they will have you put in the loony bin. In that location, your story may be more believable. So it's probably better that you and I just be secret friends."

"Walter, I think you're right," I said. "I think your theory is quite likely correct. I'm 99% certain now that I was struck by lightning. That burn on my leg is pretty good evidence of that, and I did hear your voice at the very moment that that incredible lightning struck."

"Yes, that was my voice. I was as astounded as you were by the lightning and by an apparent connection to a living person."

"I still don't know why you exist, Walter, but I guess I'll go along with what you told me until I know otherwise."

"You need some rest," said Walter. "We will talk again. Oh, and I do know about the murder in the bush."

Saturday, June 2

CHIEF PETROVIC AND Det. O'Neill boarded the train in Ottawa early Saturday morning. They were headed home to Chaseford.

They knew they had a long trip ahead of them, full of bumps and rattles and starts and stops. But this time they knew what to expect. They had even jokingly talked about taking a couple of hotel pillows with them for the trip home. Since they were lawmen, however, they realized that might not go over very well.

They were looking forward to putting the train ride to good use. They had the results of their Ottawa interviews, and there were a number of discrepancies between the statements still to mull over. Careful consideration of what they already knew would help them decide which direction to take the investigation. It was still too early to specify who the guilty party might be, but they could certainly start building a list of suspects.

The trip was uneventful until they got to the edge of Berlin, or Kitchener, as it was now called. The chief remembered the big debate in the newspapers about renaming the city 12 years earlier. The local vote at that time had been a close one, but the name Kitchener had won. Berlin, Ontario, was no more. As the train pulled into Kitchener, they began to notice debris along the sides of the track. It looked like there'd been a bad storm in the area. That made Chief Petrovic wonder what things were like in Chaseford.

The train pulled into the Chaseford Station a little after 8 o'clock in the evening. By the time they'd arrived at the station they'd seen enough of the surrounding countryside and edge of Chaseford to know that there had been a terrific storm.

The chief and Det. O'Neill debarked from the train. Det. O'Neill told the chief that he wanted to be on his way to London immediately. He was concerned about his family. He hoped London had not received as much storm damage as Chaseford had. He told the chief he would be back first thing Monday morning as he was keen to get on with the investigation.

Det. O'Neill had parked his car at the train station Thursday morning, so he volunteered to drive Chief Petrovic to the police station on his way out of town. On the brief drive to the police station, Chief Petrovic worried about his absence from town during this emergency. He hoped that Cst. Herman and Cst. Smith had been able to handle any problems that had come up.

Once the chief arrived at the police station, he went straight to his office and pushed open the door. The first thing he saw was Cst. Herman sitting in his chair. Before the chief could open his mouth Cst. Herman had sprung to his feet.

His face reddening, Cst. Herman blurted out: "Sorry, sir. I didn't know you were back in town."

"That's obvious," said Chief Petrovic, giving him a hard look. "You haven't been promoted yet, so stay out of my chair."

Cst. Herman, who detected no trace of a smile on the chief's face, apologized again.

"Tell me about the storm, Cst. Herman," said the chief, reclaiming his chair.

"There was a lot of damage, sir. No buildings were blown down, although, as you saw on your way here, the wind was excessive. There were a few trees uprooted and some hydro poles and telephone poles and fences knocked down. There were four fires caused by lightning, but they were minor and quickly controlled and put out by the fire department. The good news is that no one was killed, and, so far as we know, no one was seriously injured. We had a lightning display that was far more spectacular than anyone can recall seeing in recent memory. Some people were pretty terrified, but, like I said, no one was hurt. I think things are pretty well under control now that the storm is gone."

"Thank you for your report, constable," said the chief. "It was concise and clear. I'm going to hang around the office for an hour or so. I want you to find Cst. Smith. I want the two of you to go off duty now and get some rest. I going to give my wife a call and let her know that I'm at home and that I'm staying here for a while."

"I'm sorry, sir," said Cst. Herman. "The phones are out."

"In that case," said Chief Petrovic, "I have one final job for you, constable. I know you don't live far from my house, so would you please drop in and see my wife and let her know that I'm fine and that I'm here. I know you've been busy, and it looks like you've done a good job, so go get some rest. I need you both back here Monday morning by 9 o'clock so we can bring you up-to-date on our Ottawa interviews."

Cst. Herman apologized one more time for occupying his chair and then headed out the door.

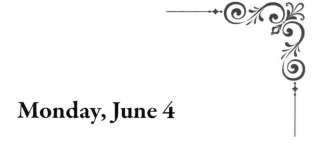

Monday, June 4

I GOT UP AT MY USUAL time on Monday. My head still felt peculiar.

I'd noticed over the last couple of days that I seemed to be more aware of things. This increased awareness wasn't particularly disturbing. It was different, but I wasn't upset by it. It was almost as if I could see more colours than I could prior to the lightning strike and my hearing range seemed sharper as well. When I was outside, I seemed to be able to hear more insects than ever. I seemed to have a greater ability to detect odours, too. I wasn't sure I liked that part as much, but I was sure I'd get used to it. When I touched things, I felt like I could finally feel the surface in detail.

I'd tried to *focus* like Walter had told me to – though I guess you might just call it concentrating, something I'd always needed to do better according to my mother and teachers – and I now found that my ability to connect with him extended beyond the attic. I seemed to be able to contact Walter anywhere inside the house and anywhere outside of it as long as I was within a few feet of it. I guess it might have depended on where Walter was, too. If I focused on Walter, and I thought a specific message, Walter was able to respond.

I no longer feared Walter. I didn't think he meant me any harm. I wasn't even sure how Walter *could* harm me. Unless I cooperated by telling people that I was in communication with someone no one else could see. What was he anyway?

I believed Walter's story. I was convinced there had been a real Walter Yost at one time. It was easy to check if I wanted to. I could go to the municipal office and find out through tax records about the farm Walter had grown up on. I would feel more comfortable if I understood what Walter *was*, though. I knew that I, Joel, was in a body and that my body moved around to different locations. The essence of Walter I didn't understand. Was he concentrated in one form in a vague shape like a ghost as described in ghost stories? Or was he able to disperse himself? Could he travel freely? Or was he tied to the house somehow? If he could travel, it would be a true out-of-body experience. I guess one way to find out would be to talk to Walter more.

However, Monday morning was not the time. I had to get back in the real world or I might miss my breakfast and be late for school. There weren't a lot of regular classes left in the school year. This year, school finished on Friday, June 29th. The last week of June would be dedicated to exams. The thought of summer coming and school ending was pretty exciting.

I'd decided not to talk to my friends about my experiences with Walter, though there might be a time when it would be necessary or appropriate. At that time, they might better understand what had happened. I still thought a lot about the body Jay and I had discovered. And I recalled what Walter had said to me late Friday night or early Saturday morning after we had had our first extended conversation: *"Oh, and I do know about the murder in the bush."*

That was another big question: How *did* Walter know? Did he know because somehow he could read my mind? Or did he know because there was some kind of connection between lost souls?

The phrase 'lost souls' seemed a little dramatic, but at the moment I didn't know what other word to use to describe these essences. It was like they were remnants of great passion stirred by anger and injustice.

"Joel, quit daydreaming!" my mother hollered. "You'd better get a move on or you'll miss your breakfast!"

My mother knew how to get my attention. She'd send me out the door partway through my breakfast to keep me from being late for school.

I put my thoughts aside and quickly finished in the bathroom and got my schoolbag together. I was at the breakfast table in less than three minutes.

My mother insisted everyone eat a good breakfast. This morning I had ham and eggs, toast, cereal, and some fresh berries from our patch in the yard beside the house. By the time I finished, I was about five minutes behind schedule. My brother Ralph and sister Emmylou had already left for school, but they had a little further to go than I did. The high school was in the same direction as the elementary school, but the high school was about five minutes closer. I still remembered how happy I was about that fact when I graduated from elementary.

On the way to school, I walked past Georgie's house. She waved at me from her front door and ran to join me. We continued down the street and after another two blocks we met up with Jay and Sylvia. We talked about the storm, a conversation that lasted all the way to school.

We were of two minds about the school and the storm. We would've hated to see any serious damage to our high school; but, on the other hand, we had been hoping that downed power lines or flooding might have delayed school for a couple of days. Our part of town seemed to have been spared most of the damage and there was little out of place on our walk. People had cleaned up their yards and the smaller debris had been moved out of the way. Sidewalks were clear, the roads were clear, and school was open.

There was a lot of talking and laughing in the halls before classes started. Everyone was really keyed up. Between the storm and school coming to an end excitement was pretty high. But when the five-minute warning bell rang everyone calmed down and headed to class.

Somehow, despite their excitement, everyone got through the school day. Mr. Graf's math class was the last class of the day and at the end he announced that he was sorry that he hadn't yet completed marking our trigonometry assignments. A power outage in his neighbourhood had prevented him from completing his marking on the weekend. He told us that, from what he had seen so far, he was pleased with our work. He told the class he would return the papers later in the week.

After school, the four of us headed for home. We all had things to do after school and wouldn't get to do our homework until after supper. My parents expected me to be at the store by 4:30 PM. My mother worked in the store a couple of hours each day to give my dad a break for lunch and errands and she usually left for home by 3:30. She would arrive home about the time that Ralph and Emmylou came in from school. My dad and I were usually home for supper sometime between 6:15 and 6:30. All in all, I had had a good day. I was still getting more information about my surroundings than I was comfortable with, but I was handling it okay.

AT 9 O'CLOCK MONDAY morning, Chief Petrovic, Det. O'Neill, Cst. Herman, and Cst. Smith were seated around the table in the chief's office.

It was time to bring the constables up to date on the information gleaned from the Ottawa interviews. As a team, they knew a lot more than they did before they had conducted their first interviews last Wednesday. It was often the case that, once all of the interviews had been reviewed, there would be obvious questions that needed to be answered. The chief, with Det. O'Neill's assistance, reviewed the Friday interviews in Ottawa for the two constables. It was easy to tell that the constables were surprised by how much the chief and Det. O'Neill had accomplished. They were also surprised by some of the responses the interviewees had given. The chief told them to hold any questions they might have until they completed the rest of their meeting.

"Our next step this morning," he said, "is to collectively think back over each interview to see if there is any inconsistency we should note. I've invited my secretary, Sherry Simpson, to come in to act as a recorder for these apparent inconsistencies. She's been sworn to secrecy."

Chief Petrovic opened his office door and called in Sherry, who arrived promptly with her notepad. When she'd seated herself, they started with a review of each interview session.

The chief and Cst. Smith started with a brief recap of the interview with Joel Franklin and Jay Jarvis. There was nothing to note from that interview. The teams then continued with their summaries of the local interviews. At the end of the discussion of all the Wednesday and Thursday interviews of last week, Sherry Simpson still had no entry on her notepad.

"The Chief and I have talked about this possibility a little bit," said Det. O'Neill. "Sometimes, when nothing arises from a series of interviews, it leads you to consider whether or not you've asked the right questions. Have you made an assumption early in the investigation that is not justified? The chief and I think we may have made such an assumption. We're just not certain whether we were deliberately misled or not."

The constables looked at them. They had no idea what that assumption could be.

"I can see that Cst. Smith and Cst. Herman are puzzled," said the chief. "Det. O'Neill, let them in on what has us confused."

"During our Ottawa interviews," Det. O'Neill started, "we came to understand that the cabin in the woods was not a secret. Nurse Bella and Proctor Carter were very aware of it. I'm certain that if we interviewed Ruth Carter and Amos Carter again, as well as the farmers who own land near the bush, most of them would have knowledge of the cabin. I'm sure Louise Carter's friends in the Chaseford area know of the cabin. I think Alice Chalmers probably visited the cabin. Many others may have visited the cabin as well."

"While I didn't know about the cabin," Cst. Smith interjected, "it seems to me that we got the impression that no one else knew about it from the boys and their families, and from Herbert and Emeline Derrigan."

"Well done, Cst. Smith," said Chief Petrovic. "That's the conclusion Det. O'Neill and I came to as well. Sherry, on your page, write down **Item 1: mystery cabin?** Then put a little arrow out to the right of the last question mark and write the name **Derrigan**."

It was time for a tea and pie break. Fortunately, Sherry had remembered to bring a pie with her to the office that morning.

"Until we conduct further interviews," the chief said when they resumed the meeting, "I see no other questions that have arisen from our local interviews of last week."

So they moved on to the Ottawa interviews. For the benefit of the constables, the chief and Det. O'Neill reviewed each of those interviews in some detail. At the conclusion of this review the chief directed a question to the two constables.

"Do either of you see any inconsistencies in what we've just told you?"

"I have a couple of comments," Cst. Herman responded. "First of all, I'm surprised by what Bella said at the very start of her interview. When she indicated that Ruth Carter had given her free range to speak about anything. I wonder if she really had that conversation with Mrs. Carter? Did she say this to gain some advantage for herself? Did she say it to steer you in a different direction in your inquiry? I also find it surprising that she never mentions knowing Amos Carter previously."

"Cst. Herman, I'm surprised," said Chief Petrovic, smiling wryly. "You seem to have a very mistrusting and cynical nature. That's a side of your character I've never seen."

"I'm sorry, sir. It's just that some of the things she said sounded too good to be true." Cst. Herman grinned.

"Well done, constable. We all need to have that aspect to our personality if we're going to be successful investigators," said Det. O'Neill.

"Sherry, get your pencil ready again," said Chief Petrovic. "For **Item 2** write: **check Bella's statements with Ruth Carter**. Below that line write: **Bella's motivation?** And below that add: **Bella's relationship with Proctor Carter?**"

"The chief and I want to avoid any more unwarranted assumptions," said Det. O'Neill. "With the aid of the Ottawa police, and in particular Assistant Chief Rutherford, we are getting a report on the businesses operated by Amos and Proctor Carter. How successful are they, really? So, Sherry, for **Item 3** note: **Carter businesses**. Also, it is apparent that some further interviews will need to be conducted with some of the people we have already interviewed, and with some of the local acquaintances of Louise Carter. A good starting point would be Alice Chalmers. Sherry, **Item 4** is: **additional interviews**."

Chief Petrovic said that he and Det. O'Neill would discuss matters further and that they would draw up a tentative interview list. He expected to conduct those interviews tomorrow, on Tuesday. With that, he ended the meeting.

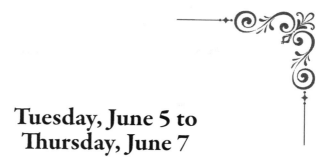

Tuesday, June 5 to
Thursday, June 7

ON TUESDAY MORNING, the chief and Det. O'Neill interviewed Alice Chalmers.

The interview confirmed their thoughts about the cabin. Many people knew about it, and Alice herself had been there several times; on several of those occasions with Louise. Alice gave them the names of five other people that she knew had been to the cabin.

On a hunch, Chief Petrovic asked her: "Do you know if Herbert or Emeline Derrigan has ever been to the cabin?"

"Yes," she replied, somewhat hesitantly.

This prompted Det. O'Neill to ask a question of his own. "How did Louise get along with the Derrigans?"

"She got along well with Herbert," she said after a pause. "Herbert helped in the construction of the cabin."

The chief interrupted. "How did she get along with Emeline?"

Alice hesitated once more. "They haven't gotten along since high school," she answered finally.

"Do you know the reason?" queried the chief.

"When they were young, Louise was kind of sweet on Herbert," said Alice. "At the time, he was Emeline's boyfriend. Emeline and Louise had a shouting match about it. That's all I know."

The chief of police decided that this was a good spot to end the interview, so he thanked Alice and she left.

"A good thing we got that information before our interview with the Derrigans this afternoon," said Det. O'Neill.

After lunch, just after 1 o'clock, the chief and Det. O'Neill met once more in the chief's office. The chief had summoned Cst. Smith to remind him that he was to go out this afternoon and talk to the local farmers about the cabin. Chief Petrovic wanted to find out what the neighbours knew about it.

"Everyone likes to gossip," he told Cst. Smith. "You're a friendly guy. I'm sure you'll get some information. Whether it's reliable or not is another question. Away you go."

After Cst. Smith left the office, the chief turned to Det. O'Neill.

"As far as I can see, we have two things to figure out before we head to the Derrigans this afternoon," he said. "The first thing concerns the Derrigans. We need to decide on the strategy we are going to use when we interview them because we need to ask them some difficult questions. The other matter involves the Carter family and Ottawa. Assistant Chief Rutherford has graciously agreed to help us with any inquiries we have in Ottawa and I want us to put our heads together to produce a list of questions for him. I understand that he has an interview scheduled with Mrs. Carter for tomorrow afternoon."

THE DERRIGANS INTERVIEWS were uncomfortable for everyone, but especially for the Derrigans. Chief Petrovic asked Emeline to wait on the front porch so that they could interview Herbert in private.

"Herbert," Chief Petrovic started, "why did you mislead us by suggesting that no one had been in that bush for years and that the cabin was unknown?"

Herbert reddened and licked his lips.

"The truth is the best policy," said Det. O'Neill.

Herbert lowered his eyes. "I do owe you an apology," he said. "Things just got a little out of control. I said those things to Joel and Jay because I was trying to scare them. So they'd understand the seriousness of going into a big bush when you have no experience. I don't think Jay's dad knows anything about the bush. He wouldn't know whether I was spinning a yarn or not. I didn't realize I was going to cause you trouble by trying to scare the boys. I just never thought any more about it."

"That explanation helps a bit," said the chief. "But I'm still bothered. Especially after I found out, through other interviews, that you helped build the cabin."

Herbert could provide nothing further of interest, so they proceeded to interview Emeline. This time, Det. O'Neill took the lead.

"Why didn't you mention that you were related to Louise Carter in the previous interview? I know we didn't ask you if you were related, but I think you would've understood that it might be relevant. What can you tell us about the relationship between yourself and Louise?"

Emeline hesitated for a moment. "We were childhood friends," she started. "Back then, our families visited back and forth a lot. My mother was a cousin of Louise's mother. For years I think we were best friends. Then high school came along and Louise and I drifted apart. As teenagers, we were interested in different things. She was more academic that I was. She had an interest in history and boys. My interests were 4-H and boys. We were still friendly, though, until grade 12, when she took an interest in a particular boy. That boy happened to be Herbert, who was my boyfriend.

"Herbert and I had started high school together, and we were already good friends before we started dating. Louise wasn't even aware of his existence until grade 12. Her interest was something I couldn't tolerate and one day, after school, she and I had quite a shouting match. It was witnessed by a lot of our fellow students. I was quite embarrassed and sorry for what had happened but Louise was made of sterner stuff. I don't think she was embarrassed at all. But I guess Herbert decided he preferred me because he walked me home that day, calmed me down, and told me he'd be my friend forever. So that day turned out to be a great day all in all.

"Louise would be civil to me when she saw me at school after that, and I would speak to her, but we definitely were no longer friends. Louise was a very clever girl but she wasn't always a considerate person. It's true that she did have some friends, but sometimes she didn't treat them very well. You should ask Alice Chalmers about that. Anyway, Louise won a scholarship to the University of Toronto where she went to pursue her interest in history. I really haven't had anything to do with her since that day in high school long ago. My mother died 20 years ago and that seemed to sever any connection I may have had with Mrs. Carter."

"Were you aware that your husband had helped Louise build the cabin in the bush?" asked Chief Petrovic.

"Yes, I was aware," said Emeline. "Herbert and I talked about it and I reluctantly agreed that he could go help. There were several people involved in building that cabin. By that time in her life, I don't believe she had any interest in Herbert, other than as someone she knew from the past who would be helpful in the construction of the cabin."

With no further questions, the chief terminated the interview. He and Det. O'Neill thanked Herbert and Emeline and left. On their way back into town, Det. O'Neill told the chief that he had another matter he was working on in London and would not be back in Chaseford until Friday.

"Not a problem," said Chief Petrovic. "There are some details for me to tidy up in this case, and there's some other police business I have to take care of. Let's plan a meeting for 9 o'clock Friday morning."

"That will be June 8," said Det. O'Neill, thinking. "I hope you don't expect me to stay late that day. It's my wife's birthday."

They both chuckled and Det. O'Neill left for London.

IT HAD BEEN A GOOD week for me. I was getting more comfortable with my new level of sensitivity and I'd had a couple more conversations with Walter. In particular, I'd quizzed Walter about whether or not he could contact any other essences. He'd said that he could, but that he'd not noticed that there were many others like him nearby. He'd told me that they weren't aware of one another unless they sent out a message. According to the limited knowledge he had about science prior to his death, he thought he and others like him must be sending out some kind of electromagnetic wave. Which explained why they didn't know who was where until a signal appeared. Even then, they didn't know the specific location of the sender unless it was included in the message. Walter had said, however, that he could tell by the strength of the signal whether the sender was nearby or far away.

"We're not noticed unless we want to be," he'd concluded. "However, it seems an involuntary signal is broadcast when a terrible event occurs. That signal goes out and those of us nearby pick it up. That's why I told you I know what happened in the bush. When that murder occurred, the person was so anguished and betrayed that a signal was emitted."

JAY, GEORGIE, SYLVIA and I were debating how we were going to celebrate the end of the school year and tossing ideas around during our walks back and forth from the school.

While returning from school on Wednesday, Georgie made yet another suggestion.

"Here's an idea," she said. "I'm almost afraid to say it, and the rest of you might not think it's a good idea, but here goes: July 1st weekend is coming up. From what I've heard my mom and dad say, everything in town is going to be closed down. There's going to be a celebration in front of the town hall at one o'clock and fireworks at nine in the park. There are some other local events planned, too. But I'm wondering if the four of us can make our own plans and have a picnic. I'm afraid to tell you the location, but my curiosity is almost overwhelming."

She came to a stop and the rest of us turned and looked at her.

"I'm talking about a picnic near the cabin in the woods," she said.

"Are you crazy?" I said. "That's a crime scene. I don't think that's going to be possible."

"My cousins near Goshawk said that the chief of police told the farmers around there that he was finished with his investigation at the cabin," said Georgie. "Though, he also told them he wasn't finished interviewing."

"We've heard you guys talk about the woods and that cabin so much that we'd like to go and see it ourselves," said Sylvia.

"I think it's a good idea," I admitted. "I just don't know whether it's possible."

"I'm glad to go along," said Jay, chiming in.

Now we were excited about the idea, though we all agreed it would be a difficult thing to set up.

"I think the first big step is to get permission from our parents," said Georgie.

"I think it will be a lot easier for us to make this happen if we work on the curiosity of our parents," said Sylvia. "I'm sure they're almost as curious as we are. I think we should consider the possibility of at least one set of parents going as chaperones. I think we should include that idea in our approach to them."

Everyone nodded in agreement. What had seemed highly unlikely only minutes ago suddenly seemed feasible.

"If our parents are in favour of the trip, it is going to be a lot easier to talk to the chief of police and the property owner," I said.

We all agreed to talk to our parents that evening.

DR. WHITTLES HEARD from Dr. Whitehead in Toronto that week but the report was not what Dr. Whittles had hoped for.

Dr. Whitehead had said that he, with the help of another forensic doctor, had ruled out the most common poisons but that they were still at a loss as to the specific cause of death. They were convinced, however, that it was a poisoning. Dr. Whitehead had said that, regretfully, he and his associate were currently involved in a number of additional cases with the Toronto police. He apologized and informed Dr. Whittles that they would not be able to spend a lot of time on a hunt for a specific poison, but that, as time permitted, they would check for other less likely poisons that may have been used.

Dr. Whittles reported this conversation to the chief of police.

"To sum up," said Dr. Whittles, "in our opinion, a murder has been committed, and the murder was committed by use of a poison. At this time, however, the specific poison has not been identified."

Friday, June 8

FRIDAY MORNING STARTED at 9 o'clock, with Chief Petrovic, Det. O'Neill, Cst. Smith, and Cst. Herman once again seated in the chief's office.

"It looks like another roundtable meeting of the Knights of Chaseford," quipped Cst. Smith.

"Except," Cst. Herman rejoined, "this table isn't round."

Realizing by the look on the chief's face that levity wasn't, perhaps, appropriate, Cst. Herman apologized.

"Sorry, sir. Cst. Smith and I are just well rested after the weekend."

"Do we need Sherry Simpson to record?" inquired Cst. Smith, changing the subject.

"Not at this time," answered the chief. "It's been a productive week, though, and we need to take a look at the new information that has come to us. But first, I'd like to welcome Det. O'Neill back."

The constables looked at the chief, puzzled.

"The London police force originally provided us with Det. O'Neill's services for two weeks," Chief Petrovic explained. "The two-week period ended this past Wednesday. But thanks to our Mayor, Det. O'Neill will be able to help us for at least another month, if necessary."

That news produced big smiles on the faces of the two constables.

"I'm going to give you copies of the notes that Sherry made from our previous meeting," the chief continued. "The first item was 'mystery cabin'. Well, we certainly cleared that up. It's definitely not a mystery cabin. From our interviews with Alice Chalmers and the Derrigans, and from the work that Cst. Smith did chatting with the farmers in the area, I'm tempted to say the only people that *didn't* know about the cabin were us. That's a bit of an exaggeration, but in that area it was very well known. If we were to take the gossip Cst. Smith uncovered as the gospel truth, you might even suppose some illegal activities have taken place there. He's quite an investigator. His friendly, smiling face and air of innocence allowed him to gain a measure of trust. The illegal activities that his investigation revealed are no longer illegal, however, with the appeal of prohibition last year in Ontario."

The light went on in Cst. Herman's head. "You mean the cabin was a good place to get a drink."

The chief nodded. "Let's move on to item two on the agenda. It was about Bella. I received a phone call from Assistant Chief Rutherford last night. He gave me a report on his interview with Ruth Carter, though he told me it was more like a conversation. He said she's a very open person. According to Ruth, she and Bella never had a conversation about Bella being allowed to say whatever she wished in the interview we conducted with her. Mrs. Carter added that perhaps Bella just understood that that would be the case. Mrs. Carter says she has nothing to hide and that Bella would know that. Rutherford's interpretation was that Mrs. Carter was trying to be kind and speaking in Bella's defence. Rutherford also reported that Mrs. Carter had had no idea that Bella knew her son Proctor. After his report on the interview, Assistant Chief Rutherford and I talked for a few minutes about Bella. We agreed that while we find her manipulative and perhaps not trustworthy, we can see no motivation behind her actions. So, for the time being, she won't be interviewed by Rutherford.

"Item three, you'll remember, was an investigation of the businesses being operated by Amos and Proctor Carter. Once again, thanks to the Ottawa police department, in particular Assistant Chief Rutherford, we received a fairly detailed report on each business and on each man. Amos Carter's survey business is legitimate it is apparently well-run and is in good standing with the bank. Amos Carter has no police record of any kind. I'll turn to Proctor next.

"From our previous discussion, you know that he operates three lumberyards. According to the bank he currently does business with, he is struggling to meet his obligations. They took him on as a customer after the bank he dealt with previously called Proctor on his loan. The only reason his current bank accepted him as a customer was because his brother Amos is a valued customer of the bank. Amos Carter sits on the Bank's Board of Directors and he agreed to provide surety for his brother."

"Things don't look good in Proctor Carter's life," said Det. O'Neill.

"There's more," the chief continued. "Proctor Carter has had three run-ins with the Ottawa police. In each case it was a drunk and disorderly. In addition, in one of those instances, he was involved in a fight. The other party, the loser of the fight, declined to press charges. All of these disturbances have taken place either inside or just outside the door of Ottawa's most unsavoury bar, 'The Tin Cup.' Based on the owners and clientele, that bar is watched carefully by the Ottawa police. The police are convinced that it's a front for illegal gambling, loan sharking, and prostitution. In Assistant Chief Rutherford's opinion, Proctor Carter either has a direct or indirect involvement in some aspect of those activities.

"We are making some progress in this investigation," Chief Petrovic concluded. "We certainly don't have all the answers yet. But we've come a long way from an unknown body at an isolated cabin. Some big questions are still in front of us. The major one is motive. The other major problem is the exact cause of death. But I'm certain we'll have answers to those two questions before a lot more time has passed."

THE FAMILIES OF JOEL, Jay, Georgie, and Sylvia had thought it would be a good idea to get together for a meeting. It was just to be the four teenagers and their parents; other relatives had been enlisted to babysit the younger children. Joel's mom had suggested the meeting after a conversation with Jay's mom, who'd come to the store for groceries on Thursday morning.

Joel's mom was very concerned. She knew that Joel had worked very hard at school this year, and she was proud of his latest achievement: Joel and Jay had received a 96% on their trigonometry assignment. This was a major accomplishment because everyone knew that Mr. Graf was not an easy marker. Joel had also worked very hard during the year at his parents' grocery store. His mother appreciated that, and she was also aware that he had been feeling a little different this last week or so. Joel never complained, but she knew he wasn't quite as easygoing as he used to be. If you took into account the murdered woman that he and Jay had found in the cabin, and added to that being struck by lightning during that terrifying storm, it seemed to Joel's mom that he deserved some kind of reward.

The meeting was taking place at Jay's parents', who had a large private rear yard. It was a beautiful yard and Friday night turned out to be a beautiful evening. It was a very pleasant place to be. Jay's mom obviously took great pride in her flowers and shrubbery.

Jay started the meeting by stating the case for the four teens.

"Joel and I often think about the cabin," he said, speaking soberly for his years. "And we always remember it with the body inside." He paused, feeling his way forward. "We don't have nightmares, exactly, but we sure don't have pleasant memories, either." The adults nodded their heads sympathetically. "We think that if we went back there for a picnic, we would remember the cabin in a different light. We would have good times to think about instead."

It was short and sweet, but it was a powerful argument and you could see the impact it had had on their parents, and on the parents of the other two teens.

"I'm a little concerned about going," said Joel's dad finally. "But I think we should do it."

"I don't disagree with you," said Sylvia's mother, "but I don't know how you're going to convince the chief of police."

"If I can get everybody's agreement, then I ask that you give me two weeks to see what I can do," said Joel's dad.

He asked for a show of hands and was pleased to see that everyone agreed with the plan.

"Just remember, you have to give us enough time to get ready for the picnic," said Georgie's mom.

Everyone laughed.

"I guess the formal meeting is over, then," said Joel's dad. "Let's dig into the snacks."

Everyone agreed to that, too.

Wednesday, June 13 and Thursday, June 14 - Ottawa

ASSISTANT CHIEF RUTHERFORD, who had many other duties, assigned one of his detectives to the Louise Carter murder investigation. He had discussed this assignment with Chief Petrovic and it had been approved by the Ottawa chief of police. He selected Det. Jean LeBlanc, who was very experienced in murder investigations. Det. LeBlanc would report directly to Assistant Chief Rutherford. Rutherford, in turn, would inform Chief Petrovic of any developments.

Det. LeBlanc had an interview set up with Proctor Carter at 10 o'clock in the morning, on Wednesday, June 13. He would not be unprepared for this interview. Det. LeBlanc had dropped into 'The Tin Cup' late Tuesday afternoon for an informal discussion with the owner, Pierre Montage. LeBlanc and Montage knew one another from a previous murder investigation: LeBlanc had caught the murderer but had been unable to connect him to Montage. Naturally, they had a mutual disregard for each other.

"You know, the police are always on the lookout for criminal activity," Det. LeBlanc said to Mr. Montage, surveying his clientele.

"Then why are you here?" replied Mr. Montage. "You should be at a crime site."

"You have quite a sense of humour," said Det. LeBlanc. "You know, we're keeping an eye on this bar. We believe it's a location where some criminal activity may be occurring."

Mr. Montage appeared to be outraged. "You have no proof of any wrongdoing at this location."

"Not at the moment," said Det. LeBlanc with a shrug. "That's not why I'm here."

"Why *are* you here bothering me, then?" asked Mr. Montage.

"I'm here to inquire about one of your patrons," the detective responded. "In particular, I want to ask you about Proctor Carter. Does Mr. Carter have any ownership in your business?"

Mr. Montage roared with laughter. "You're making a joke. Mr. Carter owes me a lot of money."

"How much?" Det. LeBlanc asked.

"I don't have to tell you, and I will not," said Mr. Montage.

"I hope you're charging a reasonable rate of interest," said Det. LeBlanc.

"But certainly," answered Mr. Montage. "I would not dream of breaking the law by charging an unreasonable rate. That would be criminal. That would be loan sharking." Mr. Montage paused. "Mr. Carter does come here with his lady friend, but that is no crime."

Det. LeBlanc thought for a moment. "Describe this woman to me," he said.

"For her age, she is an attractive woman," said Mr. Montage. "She's a brunette. A little taller than most of the women that visit my establishment. I would guess her age to be about 50. I have heard Proctor call her 'Belle'. I don't know if that's her name or if he just thinks she's beautiful."

"Are you aware of any gambling or prostitution that may be taking place in your establishment?" said Det. LeBlanc. "Are you aware if people are meeting here to make arrangements for these purposes?"

Mr. Montage once more appeared to be affronted. "Not at all, not at all. I run a legitimate establishment."

Seeing that he would get no further, Det. LeBlanc left.

Later in the day, the detective reported the details of his informal interview to Assistant Chief Rutherford. He also speculated that his visit would put a damper on some of the activities at The Tin Cup for a little while. He was sure they would now be watching for anyone who looked like a member of the Ottawa police in or near their establishment.

"Sir, I'm ready for tomorrow's interview with Proctor Carter," said Det. LeBlanc. "I believe I should also set up an interview with Bella Frankel. Since she's the good friend of Proctor Carter and the nurse caregiver to Ruth Carter, she is, I believe, certainly connected to what has gone on."

Assistant Chief Rutherford agreed. He instructed Det. LeBlanc to set up the interview with Bella Frankel for 2 o'clock, Wednesday afternoon. Rutherford then reiterated: "Keep me informed of what's going on."

PROCTOR CARTER ARRIVED at the interview room in the Ottawa police station with his lawyer at 10 o'clock Wednesday morning.

Before Det. LeBlanc could say anything, Proctor Carter said: "I can't keep coming to interviews while I'm trying to run a business."

"Well then," replied Det. LeBlanc, "let's complete this interview as quickly as we can. Who knows: if you answer all the questions to my satisfaction, we may not need another interview."

Proctor and his lawyer seated themselves.

"So, Mr. Carter," said the detective," I hear that you owe a great deal of money to Mr. Pierre Montage. I hope you understand that he is a dangerous man to do business with. I was recently involved in a murder investigation that I think Mr. Montage may have been connected to. We did arrest and convict the man who committed the murder, but, unfortunately, we were not able to get enough evidence to try Mr. Montage. Which means he remains free and dangerous."

Proctor made no response.

"I requested this interview for a number of reasons," Det. LeBlanc continued. "They are as follows: your prior charges concerning intoxication; the request for police assistance in stopping an altercation in front of The Tin Cup, where the police, when they arrived, had to pull you off a man you were beating; and the fact that you are involved in a deal with a person like Mr. Montage, whose character we've already established. This type of behaviour makes you a person of interest in the death of your sister."

"That's preposterous!" shouted Proctor, getting to his feet.

Proctor's lawyer and Det. LeBlanc both told him to calm down and sit down.

"I wouldn't hurt my sister," Proctor exclaimed somewhat less violently.

"I read the report from your first interview," said Det. LeBlanc. "From that interview, we were led to believe that you've had nothing to do with your sister or mother for many years and that you haven't spoken to them since shortly after the death of your father. I would say that lack of communication indicated a pretty substantial degree of dislike. Have you had anything to do with your sister since your father's death? Give me an honest answer. I have ways of checking."

It was a bluff that Det. LeBlanc used on a regular basis; and, in this case, he was lucky: it worked. Proctor hesitated, conferring briefly with his lawyer. The lawyer seemed to encourage him to answer.

"Well, I haven't had much to do with her," he said. "I have met up with her a couple of times."

"Why the sudden change of heart?" said the detective.

Proctor's response caught Det. LeBlanc by surprise. "Bella suggested it. Do you know who Bella is?"

Det. LeBlanc didn't want to give anything away at this point, so he simply answered "yes" with a neutral expression and then remained silent.

After about 30 seconds or so, Proctor continued. "I know you won't believe it, but I wanted to know how my mother was getting along. I was mad when my mother and Louise refused to help Amos and myself after our dad's death, but I wasn't nearly as angry as Amos was. At that time, Amos really did need the money for his business. He doesn't need it now. He's got more than all of us now. He just doesn't care about anybody. He's cut me off, too. He says if I ever approach him about money again, two things will happen: one, he won't give me a cent; and second, he will call in my notes for immediate payment and make sure I don't have anything left except the clothes on my back. That's the only reason I even thought about talking to Pierre Montage. I wish I hadn't. If I can't pay him, being in jail might be safer than not being in jail."

Det. LeBlanc thought this was worth following up. "When did you borrow the money from Mr. Montage?"

Det. LeBlanc knew this was an important question because it could establish motive. He didn't think Proctor would be aware of the significance of the question, and the detective was right.

"It was a Friday night, late in April," said Proctor.

"The last Friday in April was the 26th," said Det. LeBlanc. "Was it Friday, April 26?"

"It was," Proctor confirmed. "That's Bella's birthday and went out to celebrate. We had a couple of drinks and we got talking to Pierre Montage. Bella brought up the fact that I could use a loan. She told Montage I had three lumber companies and that my brother was Amos Carter. He pretty well handed me the money I needed on the spot. He said it was a simple deal. I have to pay him back two dollars for every dollar he gave me. The loan is due July 31st. If I don't pay, he gets my lumber companies. But Bella is shrewd. I think she outfoxed Montage. When we left The Tin Cup, Bella said to me that if we put the lumber companies in her name, then Montage will have no call on them."

Proctor's lawyer looked upset and astounded.

No wonder, thought Det. LeBlanc. *Either all the alcohol Proctor has been drinking has muddled his mind or Bella has him bedazzled.* The words "easily misled" and "stupid" came to mind but he didn't say anything.

Instead, Det. LeBlanc asked Proctor: "Do you realize what is likely going to happen to you if you can't pay your debt to Mr. Montage?"

"I have worried about that a little bit," Proctor admitted. "But I've got another seven weeks or so until the debt is due and I know Bella will figure something out."

Out of curiosity, and because Proctor seemed in the mood to talk, Det. LeBlanc probed a little further. "Does Bella have any other plans that may be helpful?"

"Bella's been very protective of me," said Proctor. "She looks after me. She managed to convince my mother Ruth and my sister Louise to include me as one of the owners of 'Bushland Farms'."

Det. LeBlanc was so amazed by what Proctor Carter had revealed in the interview that he wondered whether or not he was telling the truth. It was hard to believe that a suspect would be so candid. It made Det. LeBlanc wonder how rational Proctor was. He phoned Assistant Chief Rutherford immediately after the interview to tell him what he had found out.

Assistant Chief Rutherford was equally incredulous. His only comment was: "You'd better be able to substantiate some of this in your interview with Bella Frankel later today or we will have to seriously consider the validity of your interview with Proctor Carter."

BELLA FRANKEL WAS TALL, attractive woman with an engaging smile and a friendly manner. She was in her early 50s but had maintained a youthful appearance.

Appearances can be deceiving, Det. LeBlanc reminded himself before commencing the interview.

The detective thought he might move the interview along a little faster if he told her up front that he had already talked to Pierre Montage and interviewed Proctor Carter. Being aware of this, Bella would not be certain what information Det. LeBlanc already possessed. She wouldn't want to be caught in a lie if she was to maintain any credibility. Bella didn't know that Det. LeBlanc was already fairly certain that she was manipulative, untrustworthy, and a stranger to the truth. With these preconceptions in place, Det. LeBlanc started his interview.

He started with an easy question. "You work for Mrs. Ruth Carter?"

Bella nodded in agreement.

"Describe your relationship with Mrs. Carter," said Det. LeBlanc.

"I've worked for her for about four years," said Bella. "She's a wonderful woman. She's kind and doesn't make unreasonable demands. She's a patient woman and I respect her a great deal."

"What was your relationship like with Louise Carter?" said Det. LeBlanc.

"I liked Louise, but she could be difficult at times," said Bella. "Once she decided something, you couldn't change her mind. But we got along well."

Det. LeBlanc thought he would slip in a surprise question. "How often did Proctor Carter visit his mother?"

There was a pause. Det. LeBlanc could almost see Bella trying to determine how much he knew.

"He hadn't been to see his mother until I started working for her," she replied. "I encouraged him to come and visit her. Mrs. Carter had recovered somewhat from her stroke. I thought it would be good for both of them. It took me a couple of years to convince him. He has visited her three times in total this past year. Proctor also visited with Louise. We had to promise Proctor that Amos would not hear about these visits."

"Would it be fair to say that you and Proctor Carter are very good friends?" said the detective.

After a significant pause Bella reluctantly nodded.

"I need you to answer the question," said the detective. "I cannot accept a nod as an answer."

"Yes," said Bella.

"Bella, can you confirm that Proctor Carter is now one of the owners of Bushland Farms?"

Bella was obviously surprised.

"Do you want me to repeat the question?" said Det. LeBlanc.

"No, I'm okay," said Bella. "Yes, Proctor is now one of the owners of Bushland Farms."

"Bella, before I ask this next question, I'm going to tell you that I can easily confirm whether your answer is truthful or not, so please answer honestly: Does Mrs. Carter know about Proctor's financial predicament?"

Bella's eyes flashed. "Mrs. Carter has no idea," she replied. "She thinks everything is fine."

After the interview was completed, Det. LeBlanc immediately phoned Assistant Chief Rutherford and gave him the details.

"Congratulations, Det. LeBlanc," Assistant Chief Rutherford said. "Your interview skills are excellent. Of course, the information you obtained from Proctor Carter was very advantageous in your interview with Bella Frankel. I have a lot of relevant information here now that I can pass on to Chief Petrovic.

"Today's interviews lead me to believe that we now have one or two serious suspects in this murder investigation. I think the next step is to fingerprint both Bella Frankel and Proctor Carter and to get those prints to London for comparison to the ones they've already taken from the cups and whisky bottle that Det. O'Neill found."

Det. LeBlanc agreed.

Friday, June 15

CHIEF PETROVIC AND Det. O'Neill sat at the table in the chief's office. Chief Petrovic had arrived at about 8:30 AM from London. Their meeting with the two constables was scheduled for nine. Det. O'Neill's early arrival had allowed the chief to bring him up to date on what he had learned from Assistant Chief Rutherford about the Ottawa part of the investigation. The chief was smiling as he talked. He seemed to be in a better mood than the last time they'd met. As the chief's story unfolded, Det. O'Neill understood why the chief was a little more upbeat. It sounded like they might have a serious suspect or two for the murder.

Cst. Herman and Cst. Smith came in and took their spots at the table promptly at 9:00 AM.

"To start with, gentleman," opened the chief, "I'm going to give you a detailed report on the interviews that took place in Ottawa. That part of the investigation is now being conducted by Det. Jean LeBlanc. From everything I've heard from Assistant Chief Rutherford, and from information we received from the interviews that LeBlanc has conducted, I'm impressed and pleased that we have such a competent colleague working alongside us on this investigation."

The chief then related what new information had arisen from the formal interviews of Proctor Carter and Bella Frankel. The chief also reported the information that Det. LeBlanc had obtained in his conversation with Pierre Montage.

The chief sat back. "Does anyone have any comments?" he asked.

Cst. Smith stirred and said: "I can't believe how quickly Proctor Carter provided so much ammunition that could be used against him. He *is* a suspect, but I'm not entirely sure what his motivation would be for murdering his sister."

"Remember that with the death of his sister, Louise, there are only two owners of Bushland Farms," said Det. O'Neill. "I'm not sure what value that bush has. Would it be enough to cover the debt Proctor Carter has with Pierre Montage? We need to find out. Depending on the value of the bush it could be the motive Proctor needed to commit the crime."

"Keep in mind this is pure speculation," said Chief Petrovic. "It would certainly clinch things if the fingerprints on the whisky bottle turned out to be Proctor's, or even Bella's. I'm expecting the results of the fingerprint comparison sometime on Monday.

"I've had Cst. Herman locating and talking to as many people as he could with regard to the cabin," he continued. "So far, he's interviewed nine people who have admitted going to the cabin. In most cases, they went there to have a drink. It seems that cabin was a regular party spot on Friday evenings. Cst. Herman also found out that, with permission from Louise Carter, the cabin could be used as a convenient rendezvous for couples who didn't want their relationship known to anyone else. Cst. Herman's interview list included a couple of the neighbouring farmers."

"Don't feel bad," Det. O'Neill said to the chief. "It's not the only hideaway or speakeasy that operated in Southwest Ontario during prohibition. We pulled a lot of loose threads and unraveled a few things. There are probably still some loose strands out there."

"There's one thread that's been nagging at me ever since our last interview with Emeline and Herbert Derrigan," said the chief. "Do you remember when Emeline was talking about Louise and mentioned that she could be mean? I think Emeline said: 'You should ask Alice'. We haven't done that yet. I think we should set up an interview with Alice on Monday, Det. O'Neill.

"There is one other matter I would like to discuss," the chief said, turning to the others. "I've had a request from the parents of Joel Franklin and Jay Jarvis. As you know, those boys acted in a very mature fashion when they discovered the body. It wasn't an easy thing for them. Finding a body is never easy for any of us. Joel's dad, Arthur, is acting as the spokesperson for their families. He came to my office on Tuesday just before lunch and said he'd like to speak to me about a request that Joel and Jay had made. I was busy at the time and asked him if he could come back about 4:00. He said 4:30 would be better because his son Joel would be at the grocery store by then. He could look after things while we were talking. So we met at 4:30 on Tuesday. At that meeting he told me the families had gotten together last weekend. The two boys had told them at the family meeting that they were struggling with the memory of finding that body in the cabin. The boys suggested that if they could go on a picnic there maybe those memories of finding the body would be replaced by good memories of a happy picnic. My initial reaction was that I didn't want anybody near the place. But I didn't say anything to Mr. Franklin. My wife has told me on several occasions that if I stop and think about things for a day I'll see them from a different point of view. So I listened to my wife. I've learned by experience that her suggestion is a good one. After two days I'm beginning to think it's not an unreasonable request."

"I don't think they're going to hurt the scene," said Det. O'Neill. "I think we've found everything we're likely to find there. It's been almost four weeks since we started the investigation."

"I think you're okay to be in agreement with the request, sir," added Cst. Herman. "I just think it has to be done quietly. We don't want every Tom, Dick, and Harriet out there. I suggest, sir, that if you give them the go-ahead, that they must keep this excursion to themselves."

"They're talking about going out on the July 1st holiday," said Chief Petrovic. "That might help, because there are lots of other activities going on that day and I think most people will be involved in them. What do you think? Should I give them permission?"

The chief looked around the table and everyone nodded in agreement.

"I'll pursue this then," said the chief. "I'll pass their request on to Mrs. Carter early next week. She's the landowner. They'll need her permission."

The chief concluded the meeting.

Monday, June 18

ON MONDAY MORNING, June 18th, the chief of police's secretary, Sherry Simpson, knocked on his door.

"Chief Petrovic, Alice Chalmers is here for her 2 o'clock interview," she said.

Alice Chalmers entered the chief's office and took a chair at the table across from Chief Petrovic and Det. O'Neill. She looked quite nervous.

"Alice, we just have a couple of additional questions we would like to ask you," said Chief Petrovic. "We know that Louise's death has is been difficult for you. I think you are aware, because of the town rumour mill, that since our previous talk with you, we know a great deal more about the cabin in the bush."

They could see Alice's face take on a reddish tinge. The chief continued.

"We have interviewed many local people over the past few weeks as part of our investigation into the murder of Louise Carter," he said. "It may be surprising to you to learn that in almost every interview we gain some small piece of information that leads us to other questions. The questions take us to new interviews or back to people we've interviewed previously. Again, we get more information. That is how a case is built. That is how eventually the crime is solved and the guilty prosecuted."

Alice looked very concerned.

"We have asked you to come here today, Alice, so you can answer one such question that has arisen in our minds from a prior interview," the chief concluded, turning the questioning over to Det. O'Neill.

"In a prior interview," said the detective, "someone said that in the past Louise Carter had treated you unfairly. Why would they have said that?"

"I don't know," Alice blurted out. "I don't remember."

"I want you to calm down, Alice," said Chief Petrovic. "I want you to think about the last time you had a disagreement with Louise. I know that everyone has disagreements. Sometimes with their best friends or wives or husbands. Ninety-nine percent of the time those disputes are resolved and put aside in a short period of time. Your disagreement with Louise may have been years ago. I suspect that, since someone was aware of your disagreement, that either you've told this person about your disagreement or that they were there when it happened." Chief Petrovic could see that Alice was agitated. "I think it's time for a short break," he said. "I'll have my secretary, Sherry, bring in some tea and cookies."

A few minutes later, they resumed the interview. Alice Chalmers had calmed down quite a bit.

"This is embarrassing," she said. "I can remember the occasion that I think the other person was referring to, and I'll tell you about it, but please don't get upset with me, Chief. It happened at that cabin about four years ago."

"Are you telling us it happened when the cabin was a speakeasy?" said Det. O'Neill.

Alice coloured up again. She quietly responded "yes."

"Tell us the story," said Chief Petrovic gently.

"The cabin was open for business every Friday evening, from six until midnight," said Alice. "It was only open if weather permitted. There wasn't room for that many people inside the cabin, so most of us arranged ourselves on wooden benches or on picnic blankets close to the cabin. Louise had lots of lanterns. She enjoyed the atmosphere and would be there when she could. She was usually there once a month. She ran it like a business. My husband and I got into the habit of going to the cabin once a month, too. It was often the last Friday of every month. Louise had hired a couple of the local farmers to maintain law and order. They were imposing men and rarely challenged.

"My husband and I didn't drink much. It was an informal place to talk with people without anybody being judgmental. It was surprising for us to see 'important townspeople' there. Occasionally, someone would have a little too much to drink and there would be a minor dispute that was quickly resolved. My husband has quite a sense of humour. He doesn't use his humour pick on people. If he makes fun of anyone it's himself. The evening in question he was being quite funny. Everyone was enjoying his comedy with the exception of one other gentleman. Somehow this other man got it in his head that my husband was making fun of him. That wasn't the case, but he got quite angry. He grabbed hold of my husband and threatened him, with his fist up, ready to punch him. The two helpers stepped in and separated the men. With everyone quiet and watching, Louise then informed both of them that they were to leave immediately. I was so angered by the apparent lack of fairness that I got angry with Louise. I spoke loudly to her. As a result, I was told to leave as well.

"I'm sure that's the occasion that this other person was referring to when they said that Louise had treated me unfairly. As seen from my eyes, and probably from the eyes of anyone else who was in attendance, my husband and I were treated unfairly."

"Was this situation ever resolved?" asked Chief Petrovic.

"Within the week Louise and I discussed what had happened," said Alice. "She explained that if everyone was going to feel safe at the cabin, and if it was going to be a high-class speakeasy, then she had no recourse but to eject anybody if they were disruptive, even for the best of intentions. She apologized to me for any embarrassment my husband or I had suffered. She said we were welcome back any time. She said next time the drinks were on her. We were back to the speakeasy the last Friday of the next month. We attended regularly after that and never had another problem. Louise and I had been best friends since we were young. If anything, we were even better friends after that episode."

"Thank you very much, Alice," said Chief Petrovic. "That certainly clears up the question we had about your friendship with Louise Carter. Once again, let me say I am sorry for your loss." Then, in a teasing way, he added: "Now that you've confessed about the speakeasy, can you think of anyone else who may have held a grudge against Louise because they felt they had been ill-treated there?"

After thinking for a few moments, Alice said: "No, I can't think of anyone. I don't think anyone was permanently banned by Louise. When Prohibition ended, Louise told everyone the cabin was closed for business. She made it very clear that she didn't want anybody trespassing on the property. For the first two months after closing the cabin, Louise hired the two local farmers who had worked for her as peacemakers to attend the cabin every Friday evening until midnight. This was to ensure that no one trespassed. The first two weeks after she closed the cabin, two or three of her younger customers appeared. They were warned off the property. After that no one else came back. I can't think of anyone that would have had any reason to harm Louise." Then Alice's expression changed and she added: "I just now thought of someone from her past that was very unhappy with Louise."

The chief of police looked up from his notes. "We need you to tell us about this person. Tell us as much as you can."

"There was a man who had a romantic interest in Louise," said Alice. "She talked about him a couple of different times, when we met in Chaseford for dinner. You recall we had these best friend dinner meetings about once a year. Unfortunately, she never told me his name or where he lived. I'll tell you what I can about him. I know she met him when she was a university student. At the time she was finishing her degree and he was a young faculty member. She told me he was brilliant. He had won all kinds of awards. Louise went out on a couple of dates with him, but she quickly found out that he was self-centered and controlling. She decided she wanted nothing more to do with him and refused to go out with him again. He didn't take kindly to her rejection. He harassed her to the extent that she had difficulty completing her final year. Once she completed her degree, she couldn't wait to leave Toronto.

"He must have lost track of her or developed some other romantic interest because she didn't see him or hear from him again until after her father died. Louise told me that this man had seen her name in the paper when her father's obituary was published. Her father was such a prominent man that his death received extensive coverage. Louise received a letter from this fellow extending his sympathy to her and her family. He also requested that she meet him for a meal at Ottawa's finest restaurant. She didn't answer the letter. He sent her one letter a week for the next month. She then wrote him that she had kept the letters and that if she received another letter from him she would inform the police. She thought her problem had been solved. Then, about four years ago, she unexpectedly received a letter from him again. He told her he was friends with someone who had attended her speakeasy on a couple of occasions. Louise was terrified that he would come to the cabin. She paid her peacemakers to take a note to him. They delivered it to his residence in London. They also told him they didn't expect to see him at the cabin. I guess he got the message because I don't think he ever came. If he had, I'm sure Louise would have told me."

"He sounds like a dangerous man," said Det. O'Neill. "It's unfortunate that we don't know his name or his address. We do know he lives or lived in London, Ontario, but so do thousands of other people. Alice, if anything else comes to mind about him, no matter how trivial it may seem, you need to report it to us."

"Is there anyone else you can think of that might know about this man and his pursuit of Louise?" asked Chief Petrovic.

"I don't think so," said Alice soberly. "I was her best friend. The first time she said anything to me about this man, she made me swear not to say anything to her mother. I didn't."

Chief Petrovic and Det. O'Neill thanked Alice and concluded the interview.

That afternoon, Chief Petrovic received a phone call from the London police. They told him that the unidentified fingerprints from the whisky bottle found near the cabin did not belong to Proctor Carter or Bella Frankel.

Det. O'Neill was sitting in the chief's office when Chief Petrovic received the call. They looked at one another. They were both kind of glum. They were getting tired. They were getting lots of information, but unfortunately none of that information had led them directly to the killer.

"Just because the fingerprints don't match doesn't mean that Proctor or Bella are not guilty," said Chief Petrovic. "There's a possibility that the whisky bottle and the fingerprints on it have nothing to do with this case at all."

Det. O'Neill nodded in agreement but did not look any happier.

Friday, June 22

IT WAS THE END OF THE last day of regular high school. Excitement reigned. The only dampening influence was that exams began on Monday.

Jay, Georgie, Sylvia, and I had made arrangements with our parents that would excuse us from some of our Friday evening duties. We were heading out to the movies. This was a big event: the Chaseford Odeon Palace, the local theatre, had obtained a copy of *The Jazz Singer*. The movie was famous; it was a movie with sound, the latest innovation in entertainment. Sylvia's parents had seen it a month ago in London and they'd loved it. Hard to believe, pictures and sound together! 7 o'clock couldn't come soon enough!

There was a lineup in front of the theatre, but the four of us had arrived early enough that we knew we would still be able to get some decent seats. We saw a lot of our schoolmates there and everyone seemed to be in good spirits. The Odeon Palace was a nice theatre; it had lots of comfortable seating. I didn't get to go to the show often, but whenever I entered the theatre I was impressed by the beautiful carpeting and rugs. Georgie's older brother Robert had obtained a job as an usher at the Odeon Palace. He looked sharp tonight in his usher's outfit.

"He looks pretty fancy dressed up with that suit coat and bow tie," said Jay, speaking quietly to me.

Robert caught sight of us and escorted us to four seats about halfway down the theatre. By the time we were seated, there were about 10 minutes left until showtime.

"I'm getting hungry," said Jay, squirming in his seat.

"Be quiet," Georgie hissed. "You know you can't have anything to eat or drink in a fancy theatre. We can head to my place after the show. My mom's going to make some popcorn for us."

The lights started to dim and the organ music commenced. The screen brightened and the Movietone news came on, featuring George Bernard Shaw. This segment provided some laughter; the theatre audience was in a good mood and ready for the main event. The Jazz Singer finally started and everyone in the theatre was captivated. This stunning combination of sight and sound fully lived up to everyone's expectations. Al Jolson's singing in particular was spectacular. He performed the role of Jakie Rabinowitz exceptionally well.

Unfortunately, I was becoming extremely uncomfortable. It was sensory overload for me with my heightened senses and I knew I had to get out of the theatre. It wasn't just the film and the music, but also the noise of the crowd and the intense feelings that some of the audience experienced as they watched the show.

I was sitting beside Georgie. "I'm not feeling well," I whispered. "I'm going to excuse myself and get some fresh air."

Georgie gave me a worried look.

"I think I'll be fine," I assured her. "If I don't come back in, I'll be waiting for you outside. Please stay and watch the show. It's wonderful."

Having said that, I made my way out of the theatre.

I felt much better as soon as I was away from the crowd. I realized that it was the intense feelings of the other people that disturbed me the most. I had a feeling I would grow to accommodate these new sensations, but this reaction had caught me totally by surprise.

There was a bench not far from the entrance to the Odeon Palace, so I seated myself and thought about the last conversation I'd had with Walter.

Walter and I had agreed that the lightning strike had stimulated something in my brain. He'd encouraged me to try to focus – or in Walter's words, send a signal to him – from outside the house to see if he could receive or detect it. We had tried a couple of times with limited success. Last Saturday, on my way home from work, I had stopped about a block away from my home and focused on Walter. I thought I'd heard or felt something in response, but I couldn't make out the message if there was one. Later that evening, when I'd went up to the attic, I'd asked Walter: "At any time during the day did you detect a signal from me?"

"I'm not sure," Walter had replied. "I think I felt something just before you got home from work."

During the past week we had worked on our communication. We could now connect from more than a block away. It didn't seem that strenuous, but it did require concentration.

Walter had told me that, through signals he'd received from other essences like himself, he knew that there were other living people that possessed my ability.

"They were not all struck by lightning, though," he'd explained.

Walter and I had agreed on one basic assumption: either through accident or genetics, these other people and I were using an area of the brain that, as of yet, had been untapped by most people. Walter and I had further agreed that while a small number of these people may be in contact with essences, the majority of them were not.

"Since this happened to me," I said, "every time I read about somebody who seems to be more aware of things, or about somebody who's had a thought that resulted in a breakthrough in science, I'm convinced they're using that part of the brain that was turned on when I was struck by lightning."

"You can think it, but it's impossible to prove," said Walter.

These thoughts of the conversations Walter and I had recently had swirled through my mind as I sat on the bench. I had calmed down considerably since I'd left the theatre. It was a beautiful evening. It was still daylight and would be until a little after 9 o'clock.

I looked at my watch and was surprised to discover that it was after 8:30. The show would be out soon. I knew that The Jazz Singer was about an hour and a half long. I expected to see my friends exit the theatre in a few minutes.

At just after 8:45 my friends joined me on the bench.

"How are you?" Jay asked, sitting down beside me.

"I'm good now," I said. "I don't know what made me feel so unwell. Maybe I can't handle good entertainment."

That got a chuckle.

We sat there and talked for a few minutes. The other three were still really excited about the movie. It was the first picture show they'd seen with sound. The possibilities seemed tremendous.

Finally, Georgie said: "Let's go. My mom's expecting us."

We had a good time at Georgie's house. There was lots of popcorn, lots of soda pop, and lots of laughing.

I WAS TIRED BY THE time I got home. It had been an exciting day, but it had also been a stressful day. I was worried about the feelings I'd experienced in the movie theatre. I knew I would have to get used to this new type of situation. I would have to learn how to dampen my feelings somehow. I just didn't know how.

I went up to my attic bedroom and picked up the book I'd been reading. It was a mystery, and I like mysteries. I'd taken the book out of the library earlier in the week. It was The Big Four by Agatha Christie. I enjoyed her books and had read a couple of them before.

I settled down on my cot and just as I was falling asleep, Walter said: "Joel, are you okay? Did you try to contact me earlier tonight? I picked up a signal from you, but it wasn't the usual one we've been practising."

"I'm tired. I'll talk to you later," I said. Then I rolled over and went to sleep.

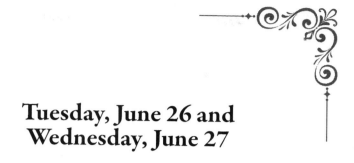

Tuesday, June 26 and Wednesday, June 27

CHIEF PETROVIC WAS sitting in his office on Tuesday morning when the phone rang. Assistant Chief Rutherford was on the line.

They launched into the case. Chief Petrovic and Assistant Chief Rutherford decided that, for the time being, they would not arrest Bella Frankel or Proctor Carter. Although they were at the top of the list of suspects in the murder of Louise Carter, the fingerprints on the wine bottle had not belonged to either of them, so, much to Chief Petrovic's disappointment, they had nothing to connect them directly to the site of the murder. The chief was somewhat concerned about Bella working for Ruth Carter and asked Rutherford if he thought Mrs. Carter was in any danger. Rutherford said that Det. LeBlanc had visited the Carter home and privately informed Bella that he was keeping an eye on her. Det. LeBlanc had reported to Rutherford that he didn't think Bella would do anything rash so long as she knew she was under his watchful eye.

Rutherford then mentioned that he had been out to visit with Ruth Carter. He said he didn't say anything about Bella or Proctor to her. When he'd arrived at the door of the Carter home, Bella had met him and acted no differently than she had on his previous visit. He told the chief that this normal behaviour had somewhat allayed his fears. When talking to Ruth Carter, Rutherford had asked for permission for the boys to go on her property. They had talked about the situation, and, although it was upsetting to Mrs. Carter, she had no concerns about giving them permission to return to the site.

Chief Petrovic thanked Rutherford for his help and said he would pass on to the families of Joel Franklin and Jay Jarvis the news that the request to visit the cabin in the bush had been approved.

That evening, Chief Petrovic phoned the Franklin home and told Arthur Franklin, Joel's dad, that they'd been granted permission to go to the cabin. Mr. Franklin thanked the chief and told him that he knew both boys would be very pleased. He went on to add that he understood that this was a private arrangement and that it was no one else's business. They were to keep their picnic a private affair.

AS WE MADE OUR WAY home from school on Wednesday, our excitement had reached a fever pitch. The four of us had written exams that afternoon. Jay and I had written grade 12 trigonometry, and we were comfortable that we had been successful. In typical Jay style, he said that it was the easiest exam he'd ever written. I thought I'd been successful, too, but I didn't share Jay's unparalleled confidence. In the same time slot, Georgie and Sylvia had written their grade 11 English final. Georgie said that it was "just an English exam, I'm not worried about it." Sylvia, who found examinations difficult, said: "I just hope I passed".

Between the relief we felt about finishing our exams and the news we'd received that morning that we had permission to go to the cabin, we were almost jumping up and down with enthusiasm. We knew we couldn't talk to anybody else about the picnic, but we certainly talked a lot to each other about it.

THAT NIGHT, WALTER and I had another conversation in the attic.

"Have you recovered from the sensory overload you received last Friday night at the theatre?" said Walter.

"Remember, this is all new to me," I said. "I'm fine now. I think I can handle that type of situation in the future. I didn't know what to expect the other night and it caught me completely off guard."

"Do you have any concerns about returning to the cabin?" he asked.

"Why would I?" I said.

There was silence for a few seconds. Then Walter said: "You need to understand that Louise is extremely upset."

"What are you talking about? Who's Louise?"

Then it struck me.

"Oh, sorry to be so slow on the uptake," I said, apologizing.

"Louise is extremely upset," Walter repeated. "She's been sending out signals several times a day. I respond to her at least once a day so she knows she's not totally alone. Maybe some other essence is responding to her as well. I have no idea. The hysteria in her communication has abated a little.

"I do have concerns about you going to the cabin," Walter continued. "With your enhanced abilities, you certainly would notice her. You might find her presence even more disturbing than the experience you had in the theatre. If you agree, I'm going to contact her tomorrow. I'll tell her a bit about you and about the picnic you have planned, and I'll tell her you will be there with other people. It's important that she understand that none of those people will sense her presence. It's important that she doesn't create a situation where your behaviour is a concern to the people you're there with."

"I'm worried about meeting her," I admitted when he was finished. "But I'm okay with your plan."

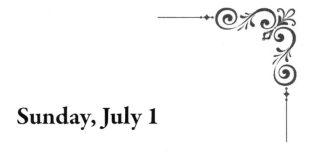

Sunday, July 1

IT WAS A GREAT DAY to celebrate Canada's birthday, a beautiful morning with only the odd fluffy cloud in the sky, and our families were looking forward to this afternoon's picnic. Most of the preparations had been completed yesterday; some things had been loaded in the car last night. The perishables would be left in the icebox until they were ready to leave home, then they would be put in hampers packed with ice.

But everyone had church to attend first.

My family and Georgie's family both attended the Baptist Church in Chaseford. It had a big and active congregation. All the members, whenever possible, attended Sunday school and church in the morning. There was also an evening service that wasn't quite as well attended. Jay's family was Presbyterian; Sylvia's family attended the local Lutheran Church. Beforehand, it had been agreed that everyone would meet at Sylvia's family's home by 1:30 in the afternoon.

Sylvia Grayson's family lived in a two-story home on a large half-acre lot near the edge of town and there was plenty of room for parking. Sylvia's mother, Clara, was a gregarious lady. She was always happiest when she was involved in preparations for some event and this picnic was an occasion she had looked forward to. She had been very pleased when they had received permission to go to the cabin. She wasn't an overly bossy person, but she loved running a picnic, and the other families had wisely allowed her to be the organizer. It was something she was good at. Clara was a kind person, so nobody's nose was out of joint about it.

It was 1:45 and all four cars were now at the Grayson home, loaded up and ready to go. There were a total of 19 people heading out to the picnic. Everyone had kept their word to the chief of police, and they had not discussed the picnic with anyone else, but as the four cars headed towards Goshawk they made a conspicuous caravan. My dad, Arthur, was driving the lead car.

"I think this procession is going to attract too much attention," I said.

"I'm concerned about it too," said my dad, "so I'm going to follow Highway 8 until we're two concessions west of the Goshawk Road. We'll turn right there and go down that gravel road. That will take us past the corner where Herbert and Emeline's farm is. At the second corner past their farm, we turn left. That's the road on the far side of the bush. It's much easier to get to the cabin from there. The others know the plan."

After hearing this plan, I was very impressed. I never really stopped to think about dad much, but I decided that, for 40, he was still pretty smart.

The four cars pulled up and stopped along the side of the road close to the **Stay Out** sign that had been posted by Cst. Smith a few weeks ago. My dad explained that the chief had told him over the phone that the sign marked the start of the trail to the cabin.

Everyone got out and stretched. The smaller kids were glad to have a chance to jump around.

"It's about a 20-minute walk," said my dad. "We're lucky it's such a beautiful day. We'll enjoy carrying everything to the picnic site. It'll be even more fun carrying it all back."

Everyone chuckled.

"We're lucky to have teenagers with us," said Jay's dad, Brad. "They're so strong and energetic."

The response was a chorus of groans from the teens, but they all loaded up and started to walk. The start of the trail was easy to find.

"I heard the cabin was a speakeasy," said Georgie. "Did all the customers walk back to the cabin?"

"Georgie, how do you know about speakeasies?" said her mother.

"I read it in the newspaper," said Georgie, smiling back.

"I heard that a lot of the customers didn't have to walk back to the cabin," said Georgie's dad. "Louise Carter had a hansom cab available for a fee. Someone told me she made more money from the cab than she did from the speakeasy."

"Oh, that was something you heard, was it?" said Georgie's mom, winking at him.

The next twenty minutes were spent pleasantly walking in the woods, with lots of chatting. Jay and I were surprised at how easy this trip to the cabin had turned out to be compared to our prior treks.

"We didn't have to mark a single tree along the way," said Jay.

My younger brother, Ralph, quipped: "There weren't any trees big enough to mark."

When we arrived at the clearing in front of the cabin, Jay and I were surprised. The open space around it was much larger than we remembered.

"I'm sure glad I brought my ball glove and bat," Ralph hollered. "There's enough room for a ballgame here."

Ralph immediately set about looking for things that could serve as bases and for the best location for home plate. Whenever Ralph appeared a ballgame was likely to break out. Some of the men picked up on his enthusiasm and helped him in his search. They knew the picnic lunch was at least an hour away. The women had already secured a couple of men to move the table out of the cabin.

Within 10 minutes, a ballgame was underway. There were nine of us playing scrub. There were three at bat and six in the field. Emmylou, at eight years old, was the youngest player. We had agreed ahead of time that no one could strike out. You were up until you hit a ball fair. The three youngest players got up to bat to start the game. Emmylou was the leadoff hitter, and she was decent. Her skills were likely due to her brother Ralph, who always had her tagging along with him to whatever ballgame he could find. On rare occasions she even got to play. These occasions only happened if all the work in the garden was done, though. Mom's rule.

We had been playing for about 15 minutes when Jay hit a foul ball down the third baseline into a small thicket of young trees. Ralph tracked the ball down and tossed it back to the pitcher. Then he said: "Timeout! Timeout, for a minute, please! There's an empty wine bottle here in the thicket!"

"Don't touch it!" I hollered.

Everyone looked at me.

"It's okay," said Jay. "Ralph, you may have found some evidence."

"I have an extra empty bag that I brought with me," said Georgie's dad. "Let's put it in the bag."

"I don't think we should touch it," said my dad. "The chief told me if we found anything out here at the cabin, we were to leave it where we found it and to let him know. I think we should just tie something colourful to the tree in the thicket close to the bottle."

Everyone agreed. The interruption got us all thinking about what had happened here and it took away our enthusiasm for the ballgame. Only Ralph wanted to continue. So Sylvia's dad agreed to hit him a few fly balls.

Since mealtime was at least 10 minutes away, I thought I'd try to sneak away for a few minutes. I hadn't sensed anything from Louise, yet. I wasn't sure whether she'd tried to contact me or not. There were a lot of people around and quite a bit a noise and excitement. Maybe she was waiting for things to calm down? I did manage to get into the edge of the bush without anyone noticing me, but I still couldn't sense anything. I tried focusing on her, but I really didn't know what she looked like. Of course, that didn't matter. I didn't know what Walter looked like, either. Then I realized that perhaps distance was a factor. I knew it was difficult for me to contact Walter when I wasn't in the house. I suddenly realized that, most likely, I'd have to be inside the cabin. That was by far the most likely place I would find the essence of Louise. So I headed back towards the cabin.

When I stepped into the clearing, Jay hollered at me.

"Where have you been?" he said. "We're getting ready to eat."

"I was on a nature walk," I said.

The meal was good and there was lots to eat. Someone had even brought a watermelon. That resulted in a seed spitting contest to the delight of some and to the disgust of others. Jay won the contest with a spit of 14 ½ feet. For reward, he got his ear tweaked by his mother. When asked if his reward had been sufficient, Jay smiled and said: "One tweak is enough."

We'd only carried enough water for drinking, so cleanup meant packing the dirty dishes away for transport home. We also carefully cleaned up any garbage we'd made. Part of our agreement with Chief Petrovic was to leave the site as we'd found it. I volunteered Jay and myself to take the table back into the cabin and make certain everything was the way it had been when we'd arrived. This would buy me a few minutes in the cabin. I wasn't alone, but if I could get Jay to be quiet – not an easy task – then I would chance a contact with Louise. My request to Jay for silence was met with a strange expression. He complied, but he said: "Joel, we need to talk about this."

"We will," I told him, "but you have to trust me for a few minutes."

Jay shrugged. I started searching for some sign of Louise.

As far as Jay could tell, all I was doing was walking around the cabin, then standing still in random places with a look of serious concentration on my face. It must have looked to Jay as though I were trying to solve some complicated math problem in my head. Jay started to say something, but I held up my hand to silence him. I did this for three or four minutes and I could tell Jay was getting exasperated. Then I heard my mom say: "Joel, we're ready to go!"

I relaxed with a sigh and shouted back. "I'm on the way."

"I want to know what's going on," said Jay. "I'm your best friend."

"Can you come over to my house tonight?" I said. "We can talk then."

"I'll come over about 8 o'clock," said Jay. "I can't stay too late. I start working for the slave driver tomorrow."

"Tomorrow's a holiday," I said.

"Not for me," said Jay. "You know my dad runs a small business. Here's how I got the job: without my being there, my dad conducted a job interview and hired me to work for his construction company all summer. I *am* a little bigger and a little stronger this year, so I'll probably avoid some of the cuts and bruises I accumulated last summer."

I smiled. I knew that, though Jay was a very clever boy, he enjoyed the physical labour, too.

"See you later," I said.

I WAS UP IN MY ATTIC bedroom, trying to tidy things up a bit. It had been a beautiful day, so as a result, my room was a little on the warm side. I heard my brother Ralph holler from downstairs.

"Joel, Jay's here to see you!"

"Send him up!" I shouted back.

About two minutes later, I could hear Jay coming up the attic stairs. Jay had visited me in the attic a few times and he loved my hideaway.

"I wish our house had a usable attic," said Jay. "This is a great place to escape from the rest of your family."

I nodded in agreement. "I love my space," I said. "I just wish it was a little cooler in the summer and a little warmer in the winter."

"Okay, pal," said Jay, making himself comfortable. "Tell me what was going on in the cabin."

"Did I ever show you where I got hit by lightning?" I said.

"Don't change the topic," said Jay. "I want to know what was going on."

"I'm not changing the topic," I said. "I'm going to show you where I got hit by lightning."

Jay shrugged. "Show me, then," he said.

"What I talk about from now on is strictly between you and me," I said. "Some of this I haven't even told my parents. But because you're my best friend, I'm going to trust you not to say anything to anybody. You have to promise that on your honour, Jay, or I'm not saying any more."

"I promise," said Jay. "So help me God."

We shook hands.

I rolled my pant leg up to the knee and showed Jay the scar from the burn on my right leg.

"That's a nasty scar," said Jay. "Is it really from lightning?"

"It sure is," I said. "Do you remember that bad storm we had on June 1st?"

"I sure do," said Jay. "It was pretty unfortunate for a lot of people. There was a lot of damage. My dad's construction company got a lot of work as a result of that storm. All the repairs haven't even been completed yet. I'm going to be working on some of those repairs this summer."

"I was home alone, here in the attic, during the storm," I said. "Lightning took out the big tree in our yard."

"I remember that," said Jay. "The first time I came here after the storm your place looked different because the tree wasn't there."

"Let me show you how lucky I was," I said, sitting on the edge of my bed. "My dad thinks a branch of that lightning hit me somehow. It went straight through my leg and then entered the steel runner on the side of my cot." I pointed. "It ran down that piece of steel, and then jumped to some other metal nearby. We don't know what."

I could tell by the look Jay gave me that he believed me. I was the only person he knew who had been hit by lightning.

"Remember your promise," I said, "because I have more to tell."

I thought for a moment. I wasn't sure how much to say and I needed to be careful. I had to have an explanation that would satisfy Jay's curiosity about what I'd been doing in the cabin, but at the same time I didn't want to get into a situation where Jay might think his friend had lost a couple of his marbles.

"I felt unwell for a couple of days," I said finally. "It was mainly pain from the burn on my leg, but my head hurt a little bit, too. I seemed to be a little more sensitive to things. I wasn't any more sensitive to your insults, fortunately, but I seemed to be able to see and hear a little better than I could before I got struck by lightning. So when I was in the cabin, I was concentrating and looking around to see if there was anything else to find that maybe someone else missed."

"What are you talking about?" said Jay.

"I think what got me so interested in looking around inside the cabin was that we'd already found that wine bottle outside. Maybe I'm just a Hardy Boy, Jay, but the more clues we find, the more likely justice is going to be done for Louise Carter."

Jay nodded. He seemed okay with the explanation. I certainly wasn't going to tell him about Walter and essences and some of the other things that Walter and I had talked about. I'd noticed the skeptical look that Jay had given me when I talked about my improved vision, so I knew I'd have to be careful.

We chatted for a little while after that about school, exams, and summer jobs, then Jay said: "You have my word." Then with a smile he added: "I have to get home now and talk to the slave driver."

"Better be good to him," I said. "Remember: he has the car keys."

LATER THAT EVENING, after everyone else in the family had gone to bed, I was sitting on my cot in the attic. I noticed that it was 11 o'clock already. It had been a good day, and I felt a lot better about the cabin now than I had before going there. I hoped I wouldn't have any more bad dreams about the body. I was still a little puzzled, though. I had expected some kind of contact or signal from Louise Carter. I didn't know what the signal would be, though. Walter and I communicated by focused thinking. Perhaps Walter would be the only one I could communicate with. I would check this out with Walter later.

I wanted to finish an Agatha Christie book I was reading. It was a very interesting mystery. I was beginning to wonder if I wasn't involved in a very interesting mystery myself. I had to get the book back to the library by the end of this week, so I settled in to read. Before I could finish two pages Walter contacted me.

Walter's first question was: "Did you learn anything from Louise today?"

"I'm not even sure that I was able to sense her presence," I said. "There was a brief moment when I was in the cabin that I thought I felt something, but it wasn't strong enough for me to be certain. Walter, have you had any communication from her about today?"

"I just received a message from her," said Walter. "She was unable to make contact with you. She said she almost made a connection when you were in the cabin with that other boy. And she was extremely disturbed when she found out that you had found a wine bottle. She thinks that this upset her so much that it interfered with her ability to contact you."

"Why would finding the bottle upset her so much?" I asked.

"Louise thinks that poison had been added to the wine in that bottle. Louise had expensive taste in wine, and she always purchased wine with the Krug label. When she arrived at the cabin that Saturday evening in May, she found a slightly chilled bottle with the label **Krug Collection 1928.** There was no card with the bottle, but she assumed it was a thank you gift from one of her Chaseford friends. Most likely Alice. She poured a glass of wine and realized too late that she'd poisoned herself. Louise still wants to try and contact you. I told her I would try to convince you to go back to the cabin sometime on your own. Louise was really pleased that the wine bottle was found. Maybe it will help in the investigation."

Monday, July 2 to
Thursday, July 5

MONDAY MORNING, SHORTLY after 10 o'clock, the chief of police was in his office doing paperwork. Det. O'Neill knocked on the door and walked in.

"I didn't expect to see you today," said Chief Petrovic. "Aren't you on holidays for a week?"

"My wife suggested a nice drive in the country," said the detective. "She wanted to see Chaseford. I think she's just checking my story about being on loan to the Chaseford police." He chuckled. "So we loaded our two boys in the car and made the journey. I dropped them off at Mabel's diner for a midmorning snack. The boys are always hungry. I told them I'd be back in about half an hour for a piece of apple pie. Is there anything new on the case?"

"As a matter of fact, there is," said Chief Petrovic. "It's really fortunate that you dropped in today. You can provide a courier service."

"You have my attention," said Det. O'Neill. "What's this all about?"

"You'll recall that we helped Joel and Jay and their families get permission to have a picnic out at the cabin," said the chief. "I received a call at 9 o'clock this morning from Joel's dad, Arthur Franklin. He thanked us very much for arranging permission to go to the cottage. He said he thought it was very therapeutic for the boys. They seemed to be in a much better frame of mind now about what they'd witnessed there earlier in May. He went on to tell me that they'd found a wine bottle in the small thicket of trees just outside the cabin. He thinks someone tried to hide it there. Mr. Franklin said no one touched it but that they'd tied a bright handkerchief to a tree nearby. They were all hoping that it would be good evidence for our murder investigation. I thanked him and sent Cst. Smith out right away to pick it up. He just brought it in about half an hour ago." He pointed to a paper bag on the desk. "He told me he'd been careful to keep the bottle upright since there appeared to be a little liquid residue remaining in the bottom. So your arrival here was serendipitous."

"Take it easy with the big words, Chief," quipped Det. O'Neill. "My translation would be that you want me to take the wine bottle back to London."

"Make sure you hand it over to the fingerprint guy," said the chief. "Tell him to handle it carefully so he doesn't spill anything. Once he's retrieved any fingerprints, please ask him to seal the bottle carefully. Then he's to return it to you. Then you will bring the evidence back here. The sooner the better. Once we have it here, I'll need to talk to Dr. Whittles."

Det. O'Neill peeked into the bag. "That's a pretty impressive label," he said. "That's an expensive wine."

ON THURSDAY MORNING, Det. O'Neill walked into Chief Petrovic's office. The chief looked surprised to see him.

"I thought you were off until Monday?"

"I received a call first thing this morning that they were finished with the wine bottle," said Det. O'Neill. "I thought I should bring it in, since you said you wanted it back as soon as possible. Also, my wife saw a couple of stores in Chaseford she wanted to visit but never got a chance to when she was window-shopping in your fair town on Monday. Besides, it's a nice day for a drive."

"Ah, so you're combining business with pleasure," said the chief.

"That's exactly what my wife said," said Det. O'Neill.

They gave each other a knowing look and laughed.

"What did you find out about the prints?" asked Chief Petrovic.

"There were several good prints on the bottle," said the detective. "They came from two different people. The one set of prints belongs to Louise Carter, which makes sense. Unfortunately, the other prints do not match anyone we have on file. They are definitely different than the prints we obtained from the whisky bottle, though. Now it appears there's another person involved."

"We seem to have a lot of trails leading in different directions," said the chief. "It's not a comforting thought. Every time we think we've found something conclusive, that's going to enable us to charge a suspect, either the evidence doesn't fit, or something else turns up to point us in another direction. I'm finding this to be a challenging case, detective."

"You know I've been involved in a lot of murder cases," said Det. O'Neill. "This is an interesting case, and one of the most challenging ones I've worked on. There *have* been a lot of twists and turns. But there is one positive thing to keep in mind about this case, and that's that we have yet to hit a total dead end. We still have evidence that needs to be checked out. We still have suspects. At some point, I'm convinced we'll find the key."

"Thanks for the pep talk," said Chief Petrovic. "I needed it today. Also, thanks very much for getting the bottle back to me so quickly. I didn't expect it back until next week. Now I need to talk to Dr. Whittles. If possible, I want him to make arrangements with Dr. Whitehead, the forensic specialist in Toronto, to check the two tin mugs, the whisky bottle, and this wine bottle for traces of what they may have contained. Dr. Whitehead may learn something significant."

THURSDAY NIGHT, AN exhausted Jay showed up at my house. He'd called earlier, saying he wanted to get together for a chat.

Jay plunked himself down on the front porch and I handed him a ginger beer.

"I'm proposing a toast to the end of summer," said Jay.

"Hold on, Jay," I said. "I'm not toasting the end of summer. We haven't had it yet."

He looked up at me wearily. "When summer ends, my construction job ends," he said. "I love my dad, but he's a taskmaster."

I looked him over. "You're looking great, Jay. You're developing muscles on your muscles."

"I thank God every day for Sunday," he said, unconsoled. "I'm here on a recruiting mission. My dad has agreed to build a driving shed for Uncle Herbert, and he wants to get it done quickly. He has lots of other work lined up, so he needs to hire some help. We'd like you to work for us on the construction of the shed. He told me he'll need you for three weeks and he'll pay you fairly. My dad's already helped you make your decision by talking to your dad. Your dad thinks it's a great idea."

I was dumbfounded. With a stunned look on my face, I said: "Do you mean that it's all been worked out and that you're just here to tell me?"

"Joel, you are so clever. You figured that out quickly," said Jay. "Don't worry about the store," he added. "Ralph has been recruited for that. Oh, by the way, you start Monday at 8 o'clock. My dad will give you a ride out to the farm."

DR. FRANK WHITTLES was smiling. It wasn't because they'd determined what poison had killed Louise Carter. It was because he finally had some additional items he could pass on to Dr. Whitehead for forensic analysis. The Chaseford chief of police had personally brought in the two tin cups, whisky bottle, and wine bottle just after lunch on Thursday and asked Frank if he would contact Dr. Whitehead.

Dr. Whittles had been very impressed by Dr. Whitehead's enthusiasm and up-to-date knowledge of equipment and procedures used in the examination of a body or of a crime scene and he'd placed the call to Toronto at once.

"I'm very pleased to hear from you, Frank," said Dr. Whitehead. "I'm just sorry that we haven't been able to help you yet. By the time we had permission for the autopsy, it was almost impossible to find any traces in the body or blood of the poison that may have been used to murder Louise Carter."

"I was very pleased that you took the time to come to Chaseford to help us," replied Dr. Whittles. "Both the mayor and the police chief have told me how much they appreciated your willingness to come to our assistance. I may have some additional things for you to examine that pertain to this case. Any help that you could give us would be much appreciated. I'm phoning to ask your permission to send to you two cups, a whisky bottle, and a wine bottle that were found near the murder site. There is still some fluid in the wine bottle that you can analyze. I don't know whether there would be any remnants of the liquids that the cups or whisky bottle had contained. If you are agreeable, we would have it driven down to your office in Toronto tomorrow."

"Thanks for giving me a call, Frank," said Dr. Whitehead. "My colleagues and I have been wondering what's been going on with that case. If you get the containers to me tomorrow, I'll hopefully have some results for you by next Wednesday at the latest."

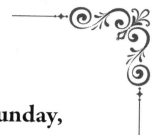

Friday, July 6 to Sunday, July 8

MIDMORNING FRIDAY, after the first customers had left, my dad and I were alone in the store. When this happens, we usually do a quick check of our inventory. It was the perfect opportunity for me to talk to my dad, but I didn't know what to say. My dad's a good man, and I'm proud of him, and he's never volunteered me for anything without talking to me first. So it was important for me to know what had happened.

"Dad, why did you volunteer me to go work for Mr. Jarvis?" I asked finally. "I already have a job here in the store. I'm used to working in a store. I'm not used to working in construction. It would've been nice if you could have talked to me first."

My dad sighed. "I feel bad about the way that it happened, Joel," he said. "Jay's dad, Brad, came into the store to buy some things on his way home last night. He was tired and he looked upset. We talked for a bit and then I said 'You seem to have something on your mind. What's the problem?' Then he told me how much work he had lined up for the summer. I told him it sounded like his business was going to be very successful this year. Then told me that he had almost more to do than he could manage, but at the same time, he wanted to keep a promise."

My dad explained how he had asked Jay's dad about the promise, and how Brad had explained that his brother-in-law, Herbert, wanted him to build a driving shed at the farm. He had promised Herbert a year ago that this summer he would build the shed. And a promise was a promise. Brad had told my dad he had a small space on his schedule starting next Monday, and he had said he could start then, but the big problem was that he didn't have enough help and he had no idea where he was going to get it at this time of year. He'd said he only had about three weeks of work for anyone he hired and he'd explained to my dad that younger guys are not going to leave their current employment to take a job for three weeks. He couldn't give them full-time work. So for the last couple of weeks, Brad had been scouting around to see who might be available. He'd said, unfortunately, the people that were available were either not reliable or not capable of demanding physical work. So Brad was in a quandary. He didn't know what he was going to do. But he was determined not to let Herbert down.

"He was desperate, Joel," said my dad. "That's when I made my mistake. I looked at Brad, and even though I knew I shouldn't say anything without asking you, I said 'I think Joel will probably help you.' I told him I could get Ralph to help me in the store. I know I shouldn't speak for you, but I told him that, unless you objected mightily, I was sure you would help him out."

"Thanks for telling me what happened," I said. "It's important for me to know the surrounding circumstances. I still would've appreciated hearing from you before Jay arrived last night. I felt uncomfortable when he told me I was going to be working for his dad. I didn't know what to say. I didn't know what else I didn't know. However, I don't mind that much. If I can help them out, I will. It's not work I'm used to, but it will probably be good for me. So I guess, from what Jay told me, I'll be picked up by them sometime before 8 o'clock Monday morning."

"I'm very sorry things happened the way they did," said my dad. "I am at fault."

THAT NIGHT AFTER SUPPER, it suddenly occurred to me: when I'm at the farm, I'm right next to the bush. I may have an opportunity to attempt communication with Louise Carter again. So I thought about how I could arrange a time to go to the cabin by myself.

I needed to get to my thinking space if I was going to figure this out, so I headed to the attic. It was quite warm up there, but it was quiet.

It's going to be very difficult to do this while I'm working for Jay's dad on that driving shed, I thought. *I can't just suddenly tell Jay and his dad that I'm taking a long lunch break – 'I'm heading to the cabin, I'll be back in a little while'.*

That would produce so many questions, first from them, and then later from my parents, that I didn't even want to think about it. But how do you get your mind to come up with ideas? I didn't know the answer and I didn't think anybody else did, either. But as I sat there, I figured something out anyway.

The next day, Saturday, when I got to the store, I said to my dad: "I could end up using my bike more this summer than I thought I would."

My dad looked at me curiously. "What do you mean?"

"Jay's dad is giving me a ride tomorrow," I said, "and that's great. But I'm certain there will be occasions when it is inconvenient for him to give me a ride. There may be times when he has to leave the site early to order supplies or to do other errands. So I think I'd better be prepared to travel back and forth to the site on my bicycle. I haven't used my bike much for the last couple of months, so I was thinking tomorrow afternoon I would travel out to Herbert and Emeline's farm. I figure I'll learn a few things from taking a trip. I'll get a look at the location for the driving shed, and – more importantly – I'll find out how long it takes me to bike out there. And where all the mean dogs live! Once I know how much time it takes me to get to the farm, I'll know what time to get up in the morning."

"Sounds like a good idea," said my dad. "I think it's about 15 miles, Joel. You should be able to do that trip in less than half an hour. But I guess you'll find out."

WE'D BEEN LUCKY THIS year; the weather had been very good. We'd had enough rain for crops, and lots of good hours of sunlight. Unfortunately for me, on Sunday it rained. It was a steady rain. The land, the farmers, and the gardeners loved it. I didn't. But I was determined to go on my bike ride.

Of course, my mother felt differently. But I guess my dad thought he owed me, because when my mother objected, he interceded.

"Mae, he's 17 years old and it's not a storm. There's no sign of lightning."

My mother relented, but before I set off on my bike, she made certain I had as much rain gear as possible. I was lucky I didn't have to take an umbrella. My dad just stood back and smiled.

"Mom, you can't tell what the weather will be," I said. "Someday, when I have to ride the bike to work, it may be raining."

"They'll probably call work off," she said.

"It depends on what we're doing," I said. "We could still work inside on the driving shed."

Reluctantly, my mother let me go. But she insisted on packing me a small emergency lunch, with a thermos of homemade juice, for my knapsack.

The ride that afternoon wasn't a lot of fun but it only took me about half an hour. And there was one positive aspect to rainy weather: most of the mean dogs preferred to stay where it was dry. I planned on going directly to the cabin; after that, I would drop in and see Herbert and Emeline Derrigan. I knew that, at some point, my mother would check with them on my visit, so I knew I couldn't spend an inordinate amount of time at the cabin. But having a packed lunch would help me account for some of the time.

When I got to the **Keep Out** sign that Cst. Smith had posted a few weeks ago, the trail was still highly visible. We had done quite a good job flattening it down the day we had had our July 1st picnic. After one quick look, I realized I could negotiate it with my bike. There were a couple of places where I had to dismount and carry the bike for a few feet, but other than that it was easy riding. The rain had slowed significantly by the time I reached the cabin. I didn't need my rain hat and raincoat anymore. I looked at my watch and noted that it had taken me 30 minutes to get there.

The cabin and the surrounding area looked the same as they had when we'd left last Sunday. It seemed that no one had been there since then. The rain had stopped, so I leaned my bike against the cabin wall and hung my rain gear on it. Then I entered the cabin and sat down on one of the chairs.

This was the test. When Walter and I communicated at home it was simple. I would just make certain I was alone. Then I would focus on him and send a message and he would respond. We communicated back and forth easily. I figured the same principles would probably be at work here.

As I sat at the table, I tried to focus on Louise. That was where my difficulties started. Until I sat there and thought about what I was going to do, I didn't realize how little I knew about her. I didn't consider my last efforts with Jay present the previous Sunday any real kind of test. I'd been too distracted. I really couldn't compare this to my first communications with Walter, either. Those conditions were created by a storm and a freak lightning strike. The odds of that happening again, anywhere, anytime, were close to zero.

I needed something to focus on. I didn't really have a good picture of her in my mind. All I had seen was the back of a dead body. I had never even seen a photograph of her. So I couldn't concentrate on what she looked like. I was at a loss, but I knew I had to think of something. It would have to be something that was common to both of us. Then I remembered there was one thing we had both seen: the wine bottle. There had been a fancy label on that wine bottle, I remembered. What was it? The name appeared to have been German. At least, I thought it was German. I remembered my dad telling me that he and the chief of police had chatted briefly about the label, and that it was the label of a very expensive wine. I think my dad had said "Krug collection 1928".

I decided that that was the message I would try to send to Louise. So I closed my eyes and concentrated on the words 'Krug collection'. I focused on the words as best as I could until I sensed something. Then I thought in my mind, the name 'Louise'. I even said her name out loud. In my mind, I repeated her name and the words 'Krug collection' over and over.

I was definitely sensing *something*, but it wasn't clear. I wasn't sure what else I could do. I tried to think of anything else I knew about Louise. I remembered that her family was famous in the area because her dad had been a Member of Parliament. His name was Hugh Carter. So I thought about 'Hugh Carter', 'Parliament', and 'Krug collection'. Suddenly, I felt my name. I could sense the word 'Joel' in my head.

I was so happy I almost began to cry. I said Louise's name out loud. There was no response, so I thought 'Louise', focusing as hard as I could. Finally, I sensed: "I hear you now".

I know that these are not real voices, and I know that Walter doesn't 'sound' like a man, but that's how I 'hear' him, even though it's not through my ears. Now I was hearing or sensing a woman's voice. The voice sounded a bit like my mother's. I was so happy.

There was a pause and I said, or thought, or sent: "Do you know Walter?"

The voice sent back: "Yes. Walter lives in your house."

"I came here because I wanted to establish communication with you," I said. "Walter told me I might be able to help you."

"God bless you," she said. "It appears we can communicate."

"I know the police are working very hard on trying to find out how you died. They are very suspicious. They think you were poisoned. Tell me what happened."

"I *was* poisoned," said the voice of Louise. "When I came here to the cabin there was a bottle of wine still slightly chilled sitting on the counter. I was very pleased, thinking that someone had planned a nice surprise for me, so I poured some into a glass. It was a warm day and I was thirsty after my trip. I noticed a peculiar taste as I drank it and was immediately frightened and suspected the drink had been doctored. Then I felt in extreme distress. I knew I was dying. I did not know who would do this to me.

"I know from Walter that the police have found some cups and a whisky bottle," she continued. "Then, last weekend, the wine bottle was discovered. I know there is something else here that is somehow connected to the wine bottle. Something has been left somewhere in or near the cabin. You must find it for me."

"Do you know anything about this object?" I responded. "Do you know how large it is?"

"I know it's connected to the wine bottle," said Louise. "I think it's some kind of personal item. I don't know anything else about it."

"I'll start my search in the group of small trees where the wine bottle was found," I said, rushing out of the cabin.

It wasn't difficult to find the right group of trees once I pictured where we had played scrub baseball. The faint outline of base paths had survived the past week and today's rain. I was thankful that the area I'd be searching wasn't very large. There were just a few trees there. I thought the best thing to do would be to get down my hands and knees, start up at one corner of the copse, and make my way in a back and forth pattern until I had completed a search of the entire area.

I began my search carefully, parting each clump of grass with my hands, and lifting each piece of undergrowth, as I scuttled on my knees in a crab-like fashion. The rain earlier in the day made certain that I would be a mess by the time I got home. I was going to have to come up with a reasonable explanation.

Good fortune was on my side. In just under five minutes I came across something of interest. It was a heavy medallion with some kind of inscription on it. Attached to the medallion was what appeared to be a gold chain, about 18 inches in length. The inscription was unreadable because the medallion was covered with mud and assorted bits of grass and weeds.

I was excited by this discovery. It fit the category of personal item, and I was certain it was what Louise and I were looking for. I was reluctant to pick it up, however. I didn't want to get my own fingerprints on it. This would have to be turned over to the chief of police.

Finding the medallion meant I could keep my reputation for honesty intact. I would not have to tell a lie to my mother. Everyone would have to know that I came out here to satisfy my curiosity, but if this turned out to be a valuable clue, I don't think my mom, my dad, or the chief of police would give me too hard a time. I needed to transport the evidence, but I had a good container for it: my knapsack. I returned to the cabin, put my knapsack on the table, and pulled up a chair.

Closing my eyes, I concentrated once more on Louise, sending her the message that I had found the medallion. She responded immediately. She was very thankful and very excited. I communicated to her that the medallion had been found in the same group of trees that the wine bottle had been located. I told her there was an inscription on the medallion that wouldn't be readable until it was cleaned up. I informed her I had to take the medallion to the police and that they would clean up the medallion and find out if the inscription was helpful. She thanked me again. She now felt certain that I had found the item that was the personal connection to the wine bottle. She told me to let her know what came of my discovery.

"I'm not sure how easy it will be for me to come back out here," I warned her. "If the medallion is a valuable clue, police may close off the cabin and the surrounding area until they're satisfied there's nothing else to find here. I'll keep you informed through Walter."

I opened my eyes, emptied my knapsack, and had my lunch. Then I took my empty knapsack back to the small group of trees and picked up the medallion by the end of the attached chain. I went back to the cabin and got my bike, and, with my knapsack over my shoulder, I headed back to the closest country road. I decided it was important for me to get back to town as quickly as I could. There would be no visit with Herbert and Emeline today.

The ride home took me just under 30 minutes. It was almost 5 o'clock when I walked through the door. I know I looked a mess: my work pants were now brown from the knees down. I had almost forgotten about my dirty clothes because I was so excited by the success of my search.

My mom took one look at me and said: "Don't take one more step. Leave your shoes outside. Ralph go upstairs and get another pair of pants for your brother." Somehow those words, and the commotion, were comforting. "Get cleaned up and come down to the table immediately," said my mother, turning to me. "Supper's ready."

My dad said grace and the food was passed around.

"We want to hear what happened, Joel," said my dad. "We want the truth."

So I confessed. I admitted that I hadn't visited Emeline and Herbert like I'd planned to, and that curiosity had gotten the better of me. I told them about searching the treed area, which explained my muddy pants. Then I told them about finding the medallion.

"We have to get that medallion to the chief of police right away," said my dad. "I'll call him at home as soon as we've finished supper."

Once supper was over and the table was cleared, Ralph and Emmylou were sent to the kitchen to do the dishes.

"You stay in the kitchen until I call you," my mother said to their retreating backs. She then proceeded to give me a good 20-minute scolding while my dad talked to Chief Petrovic on the phone in the sitting room.

When my dad had completed his call, he took over for my mother and lectured me for another 20 minutes. At that point there was a knock on the door. It was the chief of police himself.

Oh no, I thought. *I've got another 20 minutes coming!*

The chief was all business. He told me that he was disappointed I had moved the medallion.

"I apologize, sir, for moving it," I said. "I thought if I brought it back with me it would save you some time. I hoped you could start examining it first thing tomorrow morning. I was also concerned that whoever lost it might be coming back to look for it, sir."

I brought my knapsack to the table and opened it up for the chief. He took the end of the chain and carefully pulled the medallion out. He was clearly excited.

The chief of police looked at me and said: "Joel, you're forgiven for removing the medallion from the site. Hopefully, we can clean this up to make it readable. This inscription may be an important clue in our murder investigation. You may have played an important role here."

He placed the medallion in a container that he had brought with him, thanked us for contacting him so quickly, wished us a good Sunday evening, and left.

Monday, July 9

AT THEIR MONDAY MORNING meeting at the chief's office, the medallion was the big topic of conversation.

Chief Petrovic lifted it out of the box by the end of the chain and placed it carefully in the middle of the table so everyone could get a good look at it without touching it.

"It looks like an expensive piece of jewelry," said Cst. Smith.

"That's not jewelry, constable," said Det. O'Neill. "That's an award of some kind. There's a message inscribed on it. It's an impressive looking medallion."

"It certainly is an interesting discovery," said Cst. Herman. "Chief, I know you're not happy with young Joel Franklin going onto the site without permission, but you have to appreciate his determination. He was one of the boys who found the body and he obviously feels obligated to help us as much as he can."

"I was initially upset," Chief Petrovic admitted, "but the more I thought about it, the more I realized the boy had good intentions. He seems like a clever kid and he has been very helpful. Who knows, maybe he'll become a detective someday? Or maybe he's just caught up in the Hardy Boys craze. My daughters are reading those books. They have the first three in the series and they can't wait to get their hands on the latest one. 'The Missing Chums', I think it's called. They're interesting stories, but they don't provide a very accurate picture of actual police work."

"I think they're pretty well done," said Cst. Herman. "I've read a couple of them."

Chief Petrovic and Det. O'Neill looked at one another.

"Hmmm," said the chief. "Well, I think we need to talk a little bit more about the medallion. We need to clean it up so we can read the message. I want Det. O'Neill to take it with him to London today. They can examine it for fingerprints there and clean it up so the message is legible. Joel Franklin told me he didn't touch anything but the chain and I handled it the same way, so our prints shouldn't be on it. It's unlikely they'll be able to find prints, though, because there's so much dirt and other detritus on it. But a clear read of the inscription could be very helpful. The medallion was the big breaking news over the weekend. Other than that, there's not a lot to report.

"I think we need to run one more search on the murder site," he continued. "Cst. Smith and Cst. Herman, I want you fellows to go back out to the crime scene. Put up some signs indicating that no one's to go on that land until the police remove the signs. Then I want you to spend another full day doing a thorough search of the cabin and the nearby area. I don't know whether we'll find anything but we need to take another close look.

"I'm hoping there will be some more developments during the week. I had Cst. Herman drive to Toronto to personally deliver those bottles and tin cups to the forensic scientist, Dr. Whitehead, last Friday. As soon as the containers arrived, Dr. Whitehead called me. He said he hoped to have the analysis completed early on Wednesday at the latest. I'm also hoping we can get a report back on the medallion sometime on Wednesday. I'm feeling optimistic. Things finally seem to be coming together. We'll just have to wait and see what unfolds during the week. I want everybody back here at 9 o'clock Thursday morning for another roundtable meeting."

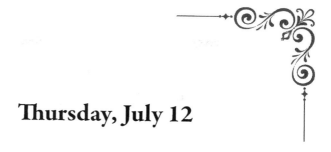

Thursday, July 12

CHIEF PETROVIC WAS up by 4:30 AM. He had received a couple of phone calls late the evening before that had prevented him from getting much sleep. He was too excited.

Tired of tossing and turning, he decided his favourite armchair in the front room downstairs was the best place for him to be. He dozed in the chair for a while, but by the time 6:00 AM came around he had to be up doing something. So he reviewed his notes on the murder case.

He jotted down a few additions to his notes and by 7 o'clock he was cleaned up and ready to go. He said his goodbyes to his family and was out the door, heading to Mabel's diner for an early breakfast. Although it wasn't really that early for some of her customers. Mabel was always cooking breakfast or baking pies by five in the morning.

It was the usual crowd. Once again there was a lot of moaning and groaning from the Indians and Tigers fans. This morning, however, there was also a bit of talk about 'The Jazz Singer', a movie he was sorry he had not attended. He still had to keep that promise to his wife. Frank Whittles, the coroner, was there for breakfast as well. On the way out, the chief dropped by Whittles's table and checked with Frank to make certain he would be attending the 9 o'clock meeting in his office.

THIS TIME, THERE WERE five of them sitting around the table in the chief's office. The chief opened the meeting by turning to Dr. Whittles.

"Frank, we'd like to hear a report on what Dr. Whitehead found out about the contents of any of the cups or bottles we sent him."

"I'll give you the abbreviated version," said Dr. Whittles. "I'm sure when the written report arrives it'll be almost incomprehensible because of all the technical, scientific, and medical words and phrases."

"I think we're all highly in favour your oral report," said Det. O'Neill.

"I'll start with the tin cups," said Dr. Whittles. "They were examined and tested thoroughly, but there wasn't a large enough quantity of any kind of residue to indicate what was in them the last time they were used."

"What about the whisky bottle?" said Cst. Smith.

Dr. Whittles turned to him with a smile. "They didn't find your lip prints on the bottle if that's what you're worried about, constable."

This comment got a good laugh out of everyone except Cst. Smith. He merely turned a nice shade of pink.

"With the whisky bottle," Dr. Whittles continued, "there was enough residue to determine that it had actually contained whisky. Whisky of a poor quality and likely homemade."

This produced some more smiles.

"Now for the wine bottle," said Dr. Whittles.

His facial expression became more serious and the rest of them knew an important statement was coming.

"There were two main components to the fluid that remained in the bottle. One of the components was indeed excellent wine from Krug Collection 1928. The other component was *Conium maculatum*."

"Please translate that for us, Frank," said Chief Petrovic.

"The common name is poison hemlock," said Dr. Whittles.

"So she *was* poisoned," said Cst. Herman.

"Apparently so," said Dr. Whittles. "When Dr. Whitehead called me from Toronto he was pretty excited. He said he'd never come across a case of deliberate hemlock poisoning in Canada. The only other cases he was even aware of were historical. The Greeks used hemlock for condemned prisoners. The most famous person to die by hemlock was Socrates."

Chief Petrovic thanked Dr. Whittles and asked him if he could stay for the next part of the meeting. Dr. Whittles reassured him that he had set his morning aside for the meeting.

"There are more revelations to come," said the chief, turning the meeting over to Det. O'Neill.

"I brought some interesting news back with me from London," said the detective. "The medallion cleaned up quite nicely. There's no name on the medallion, but it does have some significant information on it. It was awarded for outstanding achievement in the botanical research of herbaceous biennial flowering plants of Ontario. We know these prestigious awards in botany are awarded to only one person in Ontario each year. The good news is that there's a date on the medallion. It was awarded in 1912. That date proved to be of vital importance. Late yesterday, I contacted the Horticultural Society that presents the award and was able to use that date to identify the award's recipient. The winner of the 1912 horticultural award was a botany professor currently at the University of Western Ontario who goes by the name of Benjamin Frankel."

They were all too stunned to say anything.

"I was stunned, too," said the chief. "I know what you're thinking. I have been in contact with Assistant Chief Rutherford in Ottawa and we are in the process of verifying if Bella Frankel and Benjamin Frankel are related. I'm going to London with Det. O'Neill later this afternoon and we're going to interview Benjamin Franklin and obtain his fingerprints. It's quite possible that the discovery of the medallion has been a breakthrough in this investigation. This meeting is now over."

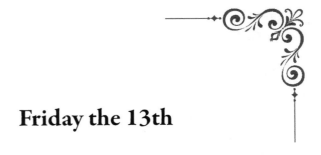

Friday the 13th

CHIEF PETROVIC LEFT Chaseford a little after 9 o'clock on Friday morning. He would be meeting Det. O'Neill at the London police station. The interview was scheduled for 10:30 AM.

Det. O'Neill had informed Chief Petrovic that when he'd contacted Benjamin Frankel on Thursday afternoon, he'd given Frankel the option to have the interview conducted at his home; a suggestion he'd said he often made if the situation warranted it. Frankel had surprised the detective by agreeing to come to the police station for the interview instead. In both Chief Petrovic's and Det. O'Neill's experience, if a suspect voluntarily goes to the police station for an interview, there's a reason he doesn't want the police at his residence, and repeated investigations had borne this out. Out of curiosity, then, on Thursday evening, Det. O'Neill had driven by Frankel's home. It was a large home on a large lot in North London. Det. O'Neill knew Frankel was a professor, but he'd said he was surprised that Frankel could afford a house that appeared so magnificent from the outside.

When Chief Petrovic got to the police station in London, he asked the desk sergeant if he would notify Det. O'Neill that he had arrived. The sergeant left the front desk and returned two or three minutes later with the detective. As Chief Petrovic and Det. O'Neill walked down the hall to the interview room, the chief said:

"O'Neill, you realize this is Friday the 13th?"

Det. O'Neill gave the chief a wry smile. "I think it's going to be a very unlucky day for someone," he said.

The two of them had about 15 minutes to chat before the interview started so they talked about Frankel's willingness to come to the station and what they thought that meant.

"I think we need to get into his home as soon as we can," said Det. O'Neill. "We have to move quickly. Which means we need to get a search warrant. But my boss, the Chief of Detectives, tells me that I don't have enough evidence to get a warrant."

"Then we need his fingerprints," said Chief Petrovic. "If they match the fingerprints on the wine bottle, I'm sure that'll be sufficient cause for anybody."

"I've been thinking the same thing," said Det. O'Neill.

"Do you serve tea and coffee here during your interviews?" asked the chief. "If you don't, now would be a good time to start."

"I think that's a good start to any friendly interview," said the detective.

Det. O'Neill went back down the hall to the sergeant's desk.

"Mr. Frankel should be here shortly for an interview," he said to the sergeant. "He's a professional-looking man in his 50s. Please prepare both coffee and tea for the interview. I want the refreshments brought to the interview room within five minutes of his arrival."

The sergeant gave Det. O'Neill a look. "Is he a special guest?"

"He's special to Chief Petrovic and me," said Det. O'Neill. "Serve the tea as soon as you can, Sergeant. Perhaps with some cookies. Then come back about 10 minutes later to collect all the cups and saucers. I want Frankel's cup dusted for fingerprints."

"Aha!" said the sergeant.

Det. O'Neill had only been back in the interview room about five minutes when there was a rap on the door. The sergeant opened the door and allowed another man to enter the room, introducing him as Benjamin Frankel. Chief Petrovic stood and introduced himself and Det. O'Neill.

Benjamin Frankel was tall, perhaps 6 foot 3, with black hair that showed traces of grey. He appeared to be healthy and in reasonably good shape. He also seemed confident. One look was enough to convince the chief that he could be related to Bella. That hadn't been confirmed yet, but he expected he would know by the end of the day.

The chief had suggested that Det. O'Neill ask the questions. The chief wanted to sit and observe Frankel's reactions. Det. O'Neill began by saying that he understood that Mr. Frankel was a university professor and that his area of expertise was botany. Frankel confirmed this.

"Prof. Frankel," Det. O'Neill continued, "please tell me about your educational career from the time you started university."

"As an undergraduate, I attended the University of Toronto," said Frankel. "I was an excellent student. Because of my top marks and my expertise in laboratory work, I then completed two years of postgraduate work at Toronto. Then I received an opportunity to work at the University of Western Ontario with an eminent researcher who was working in the field of botany I was primarily interested in. I was particularly interested in the wildflowers of Ontario. Under the tutelage of that professor, I did groundbreaking research that earned me a PhD and a prestigious medal in 1912. My innovative research has continued to this day. I'm a very focused person. As a child, I was quite gifted. I pursue something until I achieve it. That's why I've had such an illustrious career."

It was all the chief could do to restrain himself from interrupting Frankel's monologue praising his own brilliance. A couple of times, Chief Petrovic exchanged glances with Det. O'Neill. He knew Det. O'Neill was feeling the same way. The word 'megalomaniac' sprang to mind.

There was another rap on the door and the sergeant reappeared, this time with tea, which had been Frankel's preference, and a plate of biscuits. There was a brief pause in the interview while the refreshments were served.

Det. O'Neill went on to ask Frankel about his family relationships and Frankel explained that his parents had died many years ago from natural causes, just after he'd become a professor at the University of Western Ontario.

"I was the sole beneficiary of my parent's estate," Frankel continued. "They were very wealthy people. I still live in the magnificent home that I grew up in."

"Did you have any brothers or sisters?" inquired Det. O'Neill.

"I have a sister, Bella," Frankel replied. "So far as I know, Bella is my only living relative. And I don't know where she is. She was five years older than me and had no time for me when I was growing up. She was a very difficult person and caused my parents a lot of grief. She was extremely clever and manipulative. She was also very untrustworthy. They cut her out of their will after she became involved in a number of questionable situations. When they disowned her, she threatened their lives. I'm still suspicious about the manner of their deaths."

This man isn't difficult to interview, thought Det. O'Neill. *You just ask him a question and he talks until you stop him.*

"Do you have a wife or any lady friends?" the detective asked him.

"I have never married," said Frankel. "I don't have any romantic interests. There was only one woman I was ever interested in, and that was many years ago. She had no interest in me. Since then, I haven't really bothered with women."

"What was the name of the woman you had a romantic interest in?" the chief interjected.

"Her name was Louise Carter," said Frankel. "She was very clever and interesting but had no use for me. When I persisted in my attentions, she notified me that, if necessary, she would have her brothers visit me. I'm a tall man but her brothers are both bigger than I am and I had no interest in tangling with them. So I never spoke to her again."

"In answer to an earlier question," said Chief Petrovic, "you mentioned a medal that you had won for outstanding research. Where is that medal now? That medal or medallion must have celebrated an important achievement in your career. Do you have it displayed prominently in your home?"

"Yes, I keep it in my front foyer along with some other important mementos," said Frankel.

At this point the chief reached into his pocket and pulled out a small box. He put the box on the table and opened it. The medallion lay gleaming inside of it.

Frankel looked at Chief Petrovic. "Thank you very much," he said. "Where did you find it?"

The chief was surprised by his answer.

"Let me explain," said Chief Petrovic. "I was introduced to you as the Chief of Police of Chaseford and this medallion is the reason I'm here interviewing you now. It was found near a cabin in a bush owned by the Carter family. A bush not far from Chaseford."

Frankel appeared astounded. "How did it get there?" he practically shouted. He was no longer calm or confident.

Chief Petrovic was a little baffled. He hadn't expected Benjamin Frankel's reaction to be one of total confusion.

"Where were you on Saturday, the 19th of May?" he said.

"I was at Northwestern University, in Evanston, Illinois," said Frankel, still evidently perplexed. "I was there for a year as a visiting professor. I just returned to London at the start of July. I've only been home for two weeks."

Now Chief Petrovic was confused. He did his best not to show it. It was apparent that Det. O'Neill was as amazed as he was. They had both arrived at the interview convinced they had found the murderer. This, apparently, was not the case.

Just then there was a knock on the door of the interview room.

Det. O'Neill excused himself and went to the door. The sergeant was standing outside. The sergeant handed Det. O'Neill a folded piece of notepaper.

"I was told to deliver this to you as soon as possible, sir," said the sergeant, speaking quietly.

Det. O'Neill glanced at the contents of the note, then crossed the room and handed the note to Chief Petrovic.

> None of the prints taken in the case to date match the prints on the wine bottle.

Chief Petrovic glanced up at Det. O'Neill, a resigned expression on his face.

Things in this interview were certainly beginning to fit together. The problem was that they weren't fitting together the way both chief Petrovic and Det. O'Neill had thought that they would. They thanked Frankel for his time and let him go.

"Do you remember how excited we were yesterday about the discovery of the medallion and where it might lead?" said Chief Petrovic after Frankel left.

"I certainly do," said Det. O'Neill. "It hasn't taken us where we thought we would go."

"What do you think of Benjamin Frankel as a suspect?" asked the chief.

"He's an arrogant ass, but I don't think he's a killer," said Det. O'Neill.

"Nor do I," said the chief. "But it appears we were being led to think that he is."

"It certainly seems that someone – and we both know who – is trying to frame him," said the detective.

Monday, July 16

IT WAS ANOTHER MONDAY morning meeting in the Chaseford Police Chief's Office. When the meeting had broken up the previous Thursday, everyone had been very enthusiastic about the discovery of the medallion and the identification of the poison that had been used to murder Louise Carter. This morning, after the chief related the events of the Friday interview with Benjamin Frankel, there was a very different mood.

"I'm open to ideas," said the chief. "I think, from looking at the evidence we have, we all strongly suspect this is directly or indirectly the work of Bella Frankel. The biggest part of the puzzle is the evidence we have linking her brother, Benjamin Frankel, to the murder: the medallion that was located at the crime scene. That, and the fact that he is a very clever botanist who could have easily prepared the hemlock poison. But of course, he wasn't in Canada at the time that this happened, and the fingerprints on the wine bottle are not his. The fingerprints don't belong to Bella Frankel either."

"Chief, I think you're suggesting that somehow Bella Frankel obtained the medallion from the home of her brother, and further that someone else delivered the bottle to the cabin," said Cst. Herman.

"Exactly," said Det. O'Neill. "Good thinking, Cst. Herman. You do show promise."

"We need to establish that Bella Frankel was in her brother's home in London at some point prior to the murder," said Chief Petrovic. "We also need to determine who delivered the wine bottle to the cabin. Det.

O'Neill and I have talked about this. O'Neill is going to contact Benjamin Frankel after the meeting today and arrange an interview with him in his home. O'Neill wants to see the layout of the house. He also wants to find out what arrangements Benjamin Frankel made for the security of his home while he was absent. It's a magnificent house. Not the sort of house you would leave unguarded. Now," said Chief Petrovic, concluding, "let's hear your ideas about finding the person who delivered the wine bottle."

Cst. Smith spoke up. "It's not whisky, sir, but I would still be interested in finding out where it was purchased. That might give us a lead. We could also put an article in the newspaper indicating we are trying to locate someone who made the delivery to the cabin. I could go out and interview some of the farm families in the area again, too. Who knows, maybe one of them was involved?"

"Excellent ideas, Cst. Smith," said the chief. "Please follow through on them."

The meeting over, Det. O'Neill made his phone call. Benjamin Frankel, much to the surprise of the detective, agreed to have another interview with him at his home at 2 o'clock, Wednesday afternoon.

Frankel said he understood the police were just doing their job and had not been unduly upset about going to the station for the previous interview. As a matter fact, he was pleased that the police had found his medallion and relieved that it would be returned to him in due course.

Det. O'Neill inquired about the security of Frankel's home when he was absent for long periods. Frankel replied that there was an older couple in the neighbourhood, Enoch and Alma Iversen, whom he had known since childhood. They lived next door to him and had been friends of his parents. Frankel said he always had them keep an eye on the house when he was away. Det. O'Neill asked if they would be able to attend the interview as well. Frankel told him that he thought it could easily be arranged.

Det. O'Neill thanked him and hung up.

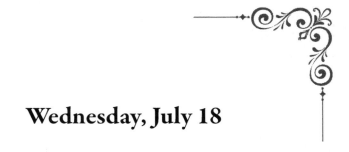

Wednesday, July 18

DETECTIVE O'NEILL PULLED into the driveway of Benjamin Frankel's North London home. It was a very impressive house indeed. This was a neighbourhood of the well-to-do, and Det. O'Neill expected a butler to answer the door. Instead, Benjamin Frankel greeted the detective personally with a welcoming smile and a firm handshake.

I had him at the police station a few days ago for a serious interview, thought Det. O'Neill, *and now he's welcoming me into his home like a friend. He's either a little different or an excellent actor.*

The front door opened onto a large, lovely, wood-panelled foyer. Across from the coat closet were two large glass display cases. Both cases had ornate wood trim matching the upper casings of the doors and windows in the grand entry. After the meeting, Det. O'Neill would recollect noting this unique pattern above all the other window and door casings in the house as well, almost like a family crest.

Det. O'Neill stopped in front of the display cases. Frankel, noting the detective's interest, proceeded to explain the significance of the items on display. After a couple of minutes, Det. O'Neill politely interrupted him.

"Would the medallion have been displayed in one of these cases?" he asked.

Frankel responded by pointing to a small, unique, but beautiful table sitting between the two larger cases.

"It was not in a display case. I had it displayed on this table with two other awards I received in the course of my career. The medallion and those two other awards were particularly important to me. As you can see, I now have a vase of fresh-cut flowers on the table. The other two awards are locked in a display case in my library. The medallion will go into the case with them when I get it back." Frankel interrupted himself. "But we'd better not tarry here. The Iversens are waiting for us in the sitting room. My maid Betsy will be serving us tea there."

Frankel and Det. O'Neill proceeded to the sitting room. It was another beautiful room, and larger than any sitting room Det. O'Neill had ever been in. Large windows overlooking the lawn let in a wealth of natural light. An older couple that Det. O'Neill judged to be in their early 80s was already sitting there. Frankel introduced everyone and his maid Betsy appeared with the tea.

They chatted politely for a few minutes, during which time, Det. O'Neill was able to assess that Enoch and Alma Iversen were sharper than most people half their age. The three of them displayed a good deal of humour and Benjamin Frankel seemed quite relaxed. He was a much nicer person in their presence.

"I understand that when Benjamin was away this past year you kept an eye on his house," Det. O'Neill said to the Iversens.

"We certainly did," said Alma. "I visited the house once a day. If I didn't come, then Enoch came and did a tour. There were never any signs that someone had tried to break in. We never noticed anything missing. We didn't realize the medallion was missing until Benjamin told us a couple of days ago."

"If no one broke in, then it must have gone missing when you were here," said Det. O'Neill.

Enoch Iversen grew angry at this speculation.

"Young man," he sputtered, "what exactly are you suggesting?" He stared hard at Det. O'Neill.

Det. O'Neill, suddenly realizing the implication of what he'd said, hastily apologized. "Please, forgive me. I wasn't suggesting that either you or Alma had taken the medallion. That was never in my mind.

Quite the opposite. I was wondering if perhaps there'd been a visitor to the house?"

Enoch, now much calmer, said: "No, I don't think so."

"There was a young woman here, once," said Alma. "I think she saw me come in because I no sooner got in the house than she knocked on the door. She said she'd gone for a walk and had started to feel a little unwell. She wondered if she could have a glass of water so she could take one of her pills. I was hesitant to let her into the house, but she told me she was a niece of Nancy Partridge. That's an older woman who lives two doors down from Enoch and me. This woman was very well dressed and I thought I recognized her. Perhaps she does look a little bit like Nancy Partridge."

"Can you describe this woman to me?" said Det. O'Neill.

"She was on the tall side," said Alma. "She may have been about 50 years old. Her hair was dark, almost black. She seemed quite pleasant. When I came back with the glass of water, she put a pill in her mouth before drinking the water. At least, it looked like she had. Oh, that reminds me: about a week later I saw Mrs. Partridge and asked her about her niece. She just looked at me and said: 'I don't know what you're talking about.' Well, I thought, that's understandable, her memory isn't what it used to be."

Det. O'Neill was convinced that the mystery woman was Bella, visiting her childhood home. And he didn't think she'd done it out of nostalgia.

"Do you think you would recognize this woman if you saw her again?" he asked Alma.

"Most certainly," she replied.

Det. O'Neill was very pleased. He was making progress.

He thanked them all for their patience and apologized if he had offended anyone. Then he stood and Frankel escorted him to the door.

At the door, Frankel stepped outside, closed the door, and turned to Det. O'Neill.

"I appreciate all your hard work, detective," he said. "But I suspect, after listening to what Alma had to say, that my estranged sister Bella is somehow involved. It saddens me, but it doesn't surprise me. I can't think of any reason why Bella would want to destroy me, but Bella is Bella."

"I can't comment on what you've just said because it's an active investigation," said Det. O'Neill. "But I can tell you I'm extremely pleased with your cooperation."

As he drove away, Det. O'Neill reflected out loud to himself: "What really happened to your parents, Bella?"

CONSTABLE SMITH TOOK on his part of the investigation with dogged determination. He liked Cst. Herman, but he also had a friendly rivalry going with him, and so far, in this case, Cst. Herman had been more successful than he had been.

There was no LCBO in Chaseford yet. Last year, with the repeal of Prohibition, the Ontario government had set up the LCBO, and there were outlets in some of the bigger cities, but London was probably the closest outlet to their area. Cst. Smith thought about going to the London location to inquire about the sale of a bottle of Krug Collection 1928. He knew that wine was exclusive enough that the purchaser would have drawn some attention. But he thought that it was a bit of a long shot because that wine could have been purchased somewhere else.

He'd been to the local newspaper office yesterday and given them the story. The Chaseford Herald was a good daily paper and had been following up on the murder investigation on a regular basis, so he expected good coverage. The story would come out in Wednesday's paper.

But he thought his best approach would be to talk to some of the people around town, the sort who had minor trouble with the law from time to time. There were always people available to deliver almost anything for a little cash. Cst. Smith had grown up in town, and his dad had been an alcoholic. He hadn't treated his wife or children kindly. In the neighbourhood Cst. Smith grew up in, this was not unusual. No doubt it was one of the reasons he'd decided to be a policeman. Cst. Smith had been lucky. He didn't suffer from alcoholism. A lot of his childhood friends hadn't been so lucky. They seemed to be repeating the cycle. Cst. Smith remembered his own past all too well and always took the time to speak to these people and to help them when he could. He was a policeman, though, and when they ran afoul of the law he would track them down.

Cst. Smith had put the word out. He'd started talking to people on the street late on Monday, but he didn't hear from anyone until Wednesday morning. He'd stopped in at Mabel's diner for a coffee just after 10:00 AM and was sitting at the counter when Johnnie Givens, a childhood acquaintance, sat down beside him.

"I hear you're looking for information about a delivery," said Johnnie. "I might know something of interest."

"Have you had breakfast?" said Cst. Smith.

"I'm always hungry," said Johnnie, grinning.

"Mabel, Johnnie here needs a big breakfast with all the trimmings," said Cst. Smith. "I'll pay for his supper, too, as long as he keeps it under $10."

"We don't have a meal that costs anywhere near that," said Mabel.

"I know," said Cst. Smith, "but he may bring a friend or family with him."

"Thanks, Billy," said Johnnie. "I won't forget this."

Cst. Smith smiled wryly. He couldn't remember the last time anyone had called him Billy. His mother used to call him Billy, but she'd been dead for 10 years.

"Okay, Johnnie, what do you know?" said Cst. Smith.

"Proofie Duncan is your man," said Johnnie.

Cst. Smith knew who Proofie Duncan was. Proofie's real name was Wallace. He got the name Proofie when he was 11 years old. At that age, he could already tell, with reasonable accuracy, the proof of any alcohol, if you gave him a taste. It wasn't the kind of nickname most people wanted their child to have, but his parents actually bragged about it. They were both dead now thanks to alcohol. It was amazing Proofie was still alive.

"Where do I find Proofie?" asked Cst. Smith.

"Try the train station," said Johnnie. "That's how he makes his money. He hangs around there hoping somebody needs something carried to the station or carried from the station to their home. About a month or so ago I was at the station talking to him. He was all excited about getting paid $20 to deliver a wine bottle somewhere. Some nice lady had noticed him hanging around asking people if he could help. They talked for a bit and when she found out that he did odd jobs she told him she had a delivery for him. That's all I know."

"Thanks, Johnnie," said Cst. Smith. "You're a big help. If this works out, I'll owe you more than supper. See you later. Enjoy your breakfast."

Good fortune was smiling on Cst. Smith. When he got to the train station, Proofie was helping some older man load some suitcases and a couple of boxes onto the train.

Cst. Smith waited until Proofie was finished then pulled him aside.

"I need to interview you," he said.

Proofie looked nervous, like he might run. "I didn't do anything," he mumbled.

"It's okay, Proofie," said the constable, "you're not guilty of anything. The chief and I just need to talk to you. We think you have some information we can use. You'll be free after the interview. We'll even buy you supper."

Supper seemed to be the magic word. Proofie relaxed somewhat and walked with Cst. Smith to the police station.

Chief Petrovic, who was fortunately available, kindly asked Proofie how he was doing.

"Come into my office," he said, "and we'll have a chat."

Proofie accompanied the police chief into his office, still a little bit nervous.

"Okay, what do you want?" said Proofie.

"We heard you delivered a wine bottle to a cabin in the bush out near Goshawk for someone back in May."

Proofie hesitated. He looked very uncomfortable.

"You didn't do anything wrong, Proofie," the chief said, reassuring him. "We're not after you. We're after some information. Do you remember what day in May it was that you delivered that bottle?"

"Honest, I didn't open the bottle," said Proofie. "I didn't drink any of it. I just did what I was paid to do. The lady wouldn't pay me until I came back to Chaseford and showed her the empty container with the ice."

"It's okay, Proofie. We know you didn't drink any of the wine."

You'd be dead and buried by now if you had, the chief thought. But he didn't say a word about that.

"Do you remember the date?" Chief Petrovic asked again.

"I sure do," answered Proofie. "That lady paid me $20. That's more than I usually make in a week. I was so excited I wrote it down in my book."

Chief Petrovic and Cst. Smith looked at one another, amazed. They didn't know Proofie could write and the last thing they expected him to have was a book. Especially considering he didn't have a permanent address.

"Where do you keep your book?" asked Cst. Smith.

"Oh, I always carry it with me," said Proofie.

"Can you show it to us?" said Chief Petrovic. This was a request he was going to regret within seconds.

"Okay," said Proofie.

Faster than the chief or constable could believe, Proofie kicked off the holiest shoes in town and took off the dirtiest socks in the county, revealing the filthiest feet in Ontario. He carried this tiny, beat-up-looking notebook in one shoe and his pencil in the other one.

Proofie was smiling. He'd known that one day his book would be valuable. He tried to hand the book to the chief, but the chief quickly declined. If Chief Petrovic had been in a bad mood, he would've told Proofie to hand the book to Cst. Smith, but luck was smiling on the constable today.

"Just show me the page with the date on it," said the chief.

Proofie pointed at May 18th.

"That's an important piece of paper, and an important date to us, Proofie," said Chief Petrovic. "If we give you another small notebook that'll fit in your shoe, and an extra pencil, can we keep this book?"

"Sure can," said Proofie, beaming. "I hope it helps."

"You've been a big help to us, Proofie," said the chief. "I'm going to tell Mabel you've earned three free breakfasts. She'll keep track for you. But please, please put your shoes and socks back on."

"Okay, Chief. But first I gotta write down three free breakfasts. That's special enough to be in my book." Proofie turned and looked at Cst. Smith. "Do I still get my supper?"

Cst. Smith smiled and said: "Of course."

"Just one last question for you, Proofie," said the chief. "Would you recognize that lady if you saw her again?"

"I would never forget anybody who paid me $20," said Proofie. And away he went, a huge smile on his face.

"Wow," said the chief of police. "We need to open some windows. You've done magnificent work today, Cst. Smith."

"It pays to know the right people," Cst. Smith said with a grin.

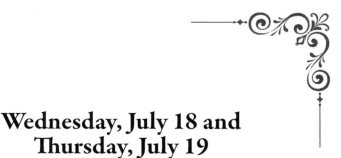

Wednesday, July 18 and Thursday, July 19

IT WAS JUST AFTER SUPPER on Wednesday. The girls had finished the dishes and Chief Petrovic was just settling in to listen to his daughters bicker. He wasn't listening closely enough to determine what they were bickering over this evening, but it was all part of the routine. He knew his wife would appear shortly and put an end to it. This evening, however, there was a slight variation: the telephone put an end to the bickering.

The chief shooed his daughters out of the living room so he could take the call in private. Det. O'Neill was on the other end of the line.

"Good evening, Chief. How are things?" said the detective.

"Normal evening," the chief sighed. "What's new?"

Det. O'Neill described in some detail the interview he had had at Benjamin Frankel's home that afternoon. Frankel had been more than accommodating, he explained, but the best part of his afternoon had occurred during the interview of Alma and Enoch Iversen. The detective sounded excited.

"What happened?" asked the chief.

"I'm certain that Alma Iversen will be able to identify Bella Frankel as a visitor to Benjamin's home during his absence in the US," said Det. O'Neill.

"That's wonderful news," said Chief Petrovic, genuinely pleased. "I have some good news, too. With the aid of Cst. Smith, we've found the person, Wallace Duncan, who goes by the name Proofie. The one who delivered the bottle of wine to the cabin on May 18th."

Now Det. O'Neill was even more excited. "Do you think we can do it, Chief?" He was referring to the issuance of an arrest warrant for Bella Frankel.

"I'm going to the County Courthouse first thing tomorrow morning," said Chief Petrovic. "I'm convinced that after today's events we have sufficient cause for the judge to issue a warrant. I'll call you tomorrow after I've talked to Judge Marshall."

JUDGE MARSHALL WAS an older man who'd been involved with the law so long he couldn't remember when he'd started. His mind was still sharp and clear. His memory prodigious and accurate. But arthritis had made it a little more difficult for him to get around.

He greeted the chief of police with a gruff "hello".

"I doubt you have anything very cheery to say to me," the judge continued. "You probably want something. That's the only time I see you, thank goodness."

The salutation, though brusque, meant the chief was in the judge's good books. Chief Petrovic knew it was the judge's brand of humour.

"What do you want?" asked the judge.

"Well, sir," said Chief Petrovic, who always used the word 'sir' with the judge. "I'm here to request a warrant for the arrest of Bella Frankel in the murder of Louise Carter." Chief Petrovic knew that the judge was always a little flattered by this sign of respect. Heaven help you if you didn't respect Judge Marshall!

"Support your request," said the judge. "I hope you have it in writing."

"Yes, sir, I do," answered the chief. "Here's what I have." He produced a document:

We know that Louise Carter was poisoned by an expensive wine to which hemlock had been added.

We know that Bella Frankel hired a local man to deliver the wine to Louise Carter's cabin in the bush. That man is innocent of any wrongdoing.

We suspect that Bella Frankel gained entry to her brother's home in London in order to steal a precious medallion. It was left near the murder scene in an attempt to cast suspicion on him. He was out of the country at the time of the murder.

We know Bella Frankel had recently manipulated Louise Carter and Ruth Carter into adding Proctor Carter's name to the company that owns the bush where the cabin stands.

Bella Frankel has also manipulated Proctor Carter into putting the ownership of his lumber companies in her name.

"We believe Bella Frankel has two motives," said Chief Petrovic. "She's a clever woman, but a very mean and nasty person. The death of Louise Carter would result in the bush land being owned jointly by Ruth Carter, an elderly woman who has suffered a stroke, and her son Proctor Carter, who does everything Bella Frankel tells him to do. Ultimately, in a relatively short period of time, the bush would belong to Bella Frankel. We also believe that Ruth Carter is currently in danger from Bella Frankel. Bella Frankel's avarice knows no end."

Judge Marshall nodded, indicating that he should continue.

"The second motive involves her brother Benjamin Frankel," said Chief Petrovic. "Upon the relatively sudden deaths of her parents a few years ago, Benjamin Frankel inherited a magnificent house and a lot of money. Bella Frankel had been disowned by her parents and inherited nothing. Sir, this motive is based on revenge, and we have forensic evidence and witnesses to back up our claims."

"Your case is not open and shut," replied Judge Marshall. "You didn't catch this person 'red-handed.' But I applaud you on your excellent police work. I will grant the warrant for the arrest of Bella Frankel on the charge of murder. She is to be held in custody at the county jail in Chaseford until a trial date is set. Go do your job, Chief Petrovic," said the judge with a smile.

Chief Petrovic was elated. This case wasn't over, he knew, but it was coming to a climax. So much time and effort had gone into this investigation, and hopefully, soon, it was going to be rewarded. He got in touch with Det. O'Neill right away.

When Det. O'Neill answered the phone, the first thing the chief said to him was: "Gerald, how about another train ride to Ottawa?"

"You got the warrant?" said the detective.

"Indeed, I did," answered the chief. "As soon as I hang up I'm going to phone Assistant Chief Rutherford in Ottawa. Hopefully, they'll make the arrest later today and you and I can pick up Bella Frankel in Ottawa tomorrow."

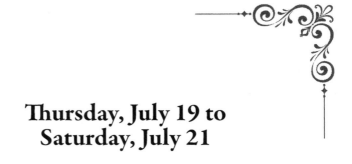

Thursday, July 19 to Saturday, July 21

THERE WAS A KNOCK ON the front door of Ruth Carter's home in Ottawa on Thursday evening. No one was expected.

When Bella answered the door, she was quite obviously surprised to find Det. LeBlanc there with two police constables. Based on her previous encounters with Det. LeBlanc, Bella Frankel both disliked and feared him. Her dislike was based on the recognition that he saw through her manipulation. Her fear was that he saw the real Bella.

"Good evening, Bella," said Det. LeBlanc. "I trust you've finished your supper."

"Mrs. Carter and I have just finished," answered Bella. "I was cleaning up the kitchen when you knocked."

Without being invited, Det. LeBlanc stepped into the house and announced: "I'm placing you under arrest for the murder of Louise Carter."

The detective promptly put her in handcuffs and read her rights to her.

Bella looked icily at Det. LeBlanc. "I was nowhere near Chaseford when Louise Carter died. You're on a wild goose chase."

Det. LeBlanc looked at her but made no reply to her comments. "Where is Mrs. Carter?" he asked instead.

"I guess you'll just have to find her, *detective*," Bella answered curtly.

A voice emerged from beyond the back kitchen. "Bella, is someone at the door?"

212

Det. LeBlanc turned to Constable Rosette McKenzie. "I believe that's Mrs. Carter's voice, constable. Please go and inform her that Bella is coming to the police station with us. Please do not mention the charges. Find out if there's anyone who can come and stay with her while Bella's gone. If no one's available, you're to stay here and assist her. I chose you to come with me today because you have experience dealing with people in her situation. Like your mother, Mrs. Carter is wheel-chair bound. It sounds like she's on the back patio. Please don't bring her into the house until after we've left."

AFTER BELLA FRANKEL was booked and safely ensconced at the Ottawa police station, Assistant Chief Rutherford phoned Chief Petrovic at his home in Chaseford.

"Things are working out smoothly," said Rutherford when Chief Petrovic picked up the phone. "We have Bella Frankel in custody. There were no problems at the Carter home when she was arrested; however, Mrs. Carter was quite upset to learn that someone she trusted completely may have murdered her daughter. She has a friend staying with her now. She'll have to make arrangements to find a new nurse; not an easy chore for a woman her age, but she does seem to have some good friends to help her. What time do you plan on arriving here tomorrow?"

Chief Petrovic thought. "It's about a 12-hour trip on a good day, and the earliest train we can catch leaves at 8 o'clock in the morning. So we probably won't arrive until 8 o'clock at night. Both Det. O'Neill and I will come to escort Bella back to Chaseford. We'll leave first thing Saturday morning. Thank you very much for all your help. Please pass a thank you on to Det. LeBlanc, too. See you in Ottawa."

THINGS WENT AS SMOOTHLY as they could. Although those train rides were never smooth.

Chief Petrovic and Det. O'Neill took custody of Bella Frankel without incident, though they did have to listen to her protestations of innocence and her accusations of police incompetence. They'd heard these kinds of comments many times before. To hear them, you'd think they'd never arrested a single guilty person. Odd how 99% of the people they arrested turned out to be guilty.

By 9 o'clock Saturday evening, Bella had entered her new accommodations. She did not seem pleased. Some people are just difficult to please. She'd get her three square meals a day, but the view did leave a lot to be desired.

Chief Petrovic and Det. O'Neill were tired. But they were pleased that they now had a suspect in custody that had a motive for the murder of Louise Carter. The final decision would be up to a jury.

"See you 9 o'clock Monday morning, Chief," said Det. O'Neill, as he pulled out of his parking space for his return trip to London.

"Do your best to convince Alma Iversen to come to Chaseford as soon as possible," Chief Petrovic hollered. "It would be wonderful if she could ID Bella Frankel."

"Will do," Det. O'Neill shouted back, waving.

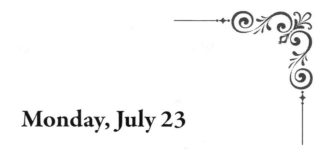

Monday, July 23

CHASEFORD WAS REALLY buzzing on Monday morning. There were rumours everywhere. The chief tried to have his breakfast at Mabel's Diner, but he gave up and left after about 10 minutes. Mabel packed the rest of his breakfast in a bag and added a piece of apple pie for him to have later. Chief Petrovic couldn't even walk down the street to his office without being pestered by questions he wouldn't answer. He wasn't happy about having his breakfast interrupted, or his walk to the office, but he wasn't going to let that interfere with the good mood that having Bella Frankel in custody had put him in.

He arrived at the office early, even before his secretary Sherry Simpson. That gave him time to finish his breakfast in peace and plan for the day ahead. Det. O'Neill arrived at about 8:45 and was soon followed by Cst. Smith and Cst. Herman.

"It's no fun being a policeman today," said Cst. Smith. "You can't walk anywhere without somebody asking you six questions you aren't supposed to answer."

"They can read about it in the newspaper," said Chief Petrovic. "We're having this meeting today to make sure we all have the same information and haven't accidentally been infected by any outside rumours. There will be a press release late this afternoon.

"Det. O'Neill tells me that Alva and Enoch Iversen will be here by 2:00. Apparently, Enoch Iversen has a new Model A Ford Town Car he likes to show off. It's a beautiful car and he drives it whenever he can, so he's looking forward to his trip to Chaseford. Remember, his wife Al-

215

ma is the woman who can identify Bella Frankel and confirm that she
was in her brother's home in London earlier this year. We suspect that
that's when Bella took the medallion to frame her brother, Benjamin
Frankel. Cst. Smith has assured me that Proofie Duncan will be here as
well to identify Bella. Bella Frankel maintains that she is innocent and
has hired a top-flight criminal lawyer from Ottawa to handle her case.
Her lawyer has already requested a bail hearing. I doubt very much that
the judge will allow her bail because of the risk to Ruth Carter."

THE IVERSEN'S ARRIVED at the police station shortly before 2
o'clock. Enoch, excited to be part of the investigation, couldn't stop
talking about his new Model A Ford.

Alma, however, was nervous and just wanted to get it over with.
She wasn't afraid of seeing Bella; she was angry for having been tricked
by her back in the spring. She complained to the chief that she didn't
like it when people lied to her. Chief Petrovic wondered if he would
have to protect Bella from Alma.

Cst. Smith brought Proofie into the station shortly after the
Iversen's arrived. Proofie was wearing a new shirt, but he still had on the
same shoes and socks. Chief Petrovic was certain the new pad he had
given him was in the bottom of his left shoe. Proofie was excited about
being in the police station when he had done nothing wrong. It was a
new experience for him.

The chief of police was proud of the one-way mirror that had been
installed in the station a year ago. This wouldn't be the first time it had
been used for identification purposes, but it would be the first time it
had been used in a prominent murder investigation in Chaseford. Both
Alma Iversen and Proofie Duncan identified Bella Frankel without hes-
itation.

Chief Petrovic and Det. O'Neill could now give a genuine sigh of relief. The local prosecutor was ecstatic. This case was now in the hands of the law.

The Rest of the Story - Thursday, October 25, 1928

THE TRIAL ENDED YESTERDAY and now Jay and I are local heroes. We didn't intend to be; but as the trial wore on, and our exploits were mentioned, we became locally famous, and even somewhat known in the province of Ontario.

The trial was intriguing to the newspaper people because it involved the daughter of a beloved politician and a mysterious woman from Ottawa. From the first day of the trial to the final day and the jury's verdict the town of Chaseford was packed with visitors. All the prominent Canadian papers had representation at the trial as well as the New York Times and the London Observer. The town was so busy that Mabel had to hire extra staff for the diner. During the course of the trial, Jay and I were mentioned several times: first, in regard to stumbling across the body, and then again when we stumbled across the wine bottle and the medallion. This led to several interviews, which we also stumbled our way through.

I attended as much of the trial as I could. My parents have been kind enough to give me time off work at the store. The store's business has improved as well. It seems everyone wants to come in and talk about the trial of Bella Frankel.

School's back in, of course, and Jay and I are in Grade 13. It's our final year of high school so there are some big decisions ahead of us. I'm not sure what I'm going to do. My parents have told me that they will do their best to make certain I get the best education I can. I know my mom really wants me to go to the University of Western Ontario. After this summer, I have become very interested in pursuing a career in the law. I'm not certain yet whether there are any universities that offer programs in criminology. I know there are courses at the University of Chicago. I guess mom and I will just have to wait and see what happens. I still have to finish my grade 13 year successfully.

With notes from our parents, the high school principal reluctantly allowed Jay and I to miss school yesterday so that we could attend the final day of the trial. The closing arguments had been presented the previous day. By midafternoon, the jury had been instructed. Most reporters didn't expect the jury to be out long. Although Bella Frankel was an attractive woman, her aloof manner didn't sit well with the jurors. The evidence, although circumstantial, along with the testimony of the other parties, painted a picture of a cruel and manipulative woman who would do anything to achieve her goals. Not only was it implied that she had murdered a woman who was well-liked, but she showed no interest or concern for the deceased.

At 10:30 in the morning on Wednesday, October 24, the jury returned to the courtroom. Judge Marshall asked the jury foreman if they had reached a verdict.

The foreman responded: "Yes, Your Honour. We are of one mind. The vote is 12 to 0 in favour of the charge of first-degree murder."

The courtroom erupted with a surge of positive comments. The lone exception was the loud, strident voice of Bella Frankel.

"This is outrageous!" she shouted. "This is a travesty of justice!"

Judge Marshall pounded his gavel and demanded order in the court. The courtroom fell deathly silent. Everyone knew Judge Marshall was quick to remove anyone who didn't comply with his wishes immediately.

"Bella Frankel," said Judge Marshall. "I have thought at length during this trial about the sentence you should receive and I see no point in delaying your sentencing. You are hereby sentenced to death by hanging for the murder of Louise Carter."

Bella rose to object but her lawyer told her to be quiet. He turned to the judge and said: "Your Honour, with all due respect to your determination, we shall proceed with an appeal at the earliest possible date."

"Court dismissed," said Judge Marshall.

"WHAT DO YOU THINK, Joel?" Jay said when we got out of the courtroom.

"I have no doubt that she's guilty," I said, "and she deserves full punishment for the murder, but I'm not sure I agree with the death penalty."

"I think she deserves the death penalty," said Jay, unmoved.

This was a debate that had been going on in the community since the start of the trial, long before the verdict was reached.

JAY AND I RECEIVED special medallions for our contributions to the successful conclusion of this high-profile murder investigation. These medallions were presented by the mayor at a New Year's Day community celebration.

My mom and I agreed that I would attend the University of Western Ontario and I enrolled in the fall of 1929. Even though Jay was the top academic student in his class, he had decided not to continue with schooling at this time. His father had suffered a significant leg injury late in the fall of 1928. Once Jay completed his grade 13 year, he took over as the on-site manager for his dad's small construction company.

Chief Petrovic and Det. O'Neill received commendations for their excellent police work from the mayor of Chaseford at the New Year's Gala, and Cst. Jake Smith and Cst. Peter Herman received special commendations from Chief Petrovic. They both received an increase in salary, and they both want to become detectives.

Bella Frankel is currently incarcerated and is still facing the death penalty. She still maintains that she is innocent. Her appeal is ongoing.

Ruth Carter has survived the death of her only daughter and the betrayal of her former nurse and supposed friend Bella Frankel. Mrs. Carter has a new live-in nurse. Her son Proctor now lives with her as well and is a recovering alcoholic. With the aid of his mother's financing, and a good lawyer, he has recovered the ownership of his lumber companies. They are doing well. After an extended Ottawa police station interview with Det. Jean LeBlanc and Assistant Chief Rutherford, Pierre Montage has generously decided to forgive Proctor Carter his debt.

Amos Carter will still have nothing to do with this mother Ruth or his brother Proctor.

Walter Yost and I still have lengthy conversations in my attic and we are continuing to work on our focusing abilities. Walter and I can now communicate with each other up to distances of one mile. That's probably the limit, and I don't think we could do that in a city. By the time I finished grade 13, we had made contact with two other essences in the region.

The end ... for now

About the Author

Many years ago, when I was three, my mother took me to the library. She was delighted that I loved to read. My father was not so happy. He knew books would cut into chore time.

He was right.

I read and I read and I read and I read. Even today I'm reading. And recently I decided to write.

Lightning at 200 Durham Street, and *Where's the Rest of the Body?* are the first two books in the Joel Franklin Mystery series, but there are many more on the way.

Stay tuned.

37727616R00128

Made in the USA
Middletown, DE
01 March 2019